Dead and Kicking

The Harry Russo Diaries, volume 1

By Lisa Emme

Dead and Kicking
The Harry Russo Diaries, vol. 1

Copyright 2015 Lisa Emme

Print Edition
ISBN 978-0-9948288-0-4
All rights reserved.

Cover design by
Scarlett Rugers Design
www.scarlettrugers.com

This book is a work of fiction. Names, characters, places, and incidents are products of the author's wild and crazy imagination or are used fictitiously. Any resemblance to actual persons, living or dead, events, or locales is entirely coincidental.

Visit Lisa at

www.lisaemme.com

To my son, Quinn
You are my greatest creation
This is just a book.

And to my big brother, Scott
For inspiring me with your
Strength and courage
And reminding me that
There's no time to waste.
This is me, throwing off the bowlines.

Chapter One

"Not that one," Gran said with an exaggerated sigh as I held up one dress and then another. "Not that one either." The offending dresses joined the growing pile of rejects on the bed.

"This is ridiculous," I replied. "This whole thing is ridiculous." I stomped back to my closet to try again. I mentally tried on one outfit after another, the hangers zinging back and forth along the rod, as I attempted to find something that would pass Gran's inspection. "I can't believe I let you talk me into this."

"Don't get your panties in a twist. It's just a coffee date, not an arranged marriage."

"It's not even a date! It's an ambush." Zing, zing, zing, the hangers continued to fly back and forth. Finally my hand fell on a cute, little sun dress, paired with a sweater to keep away the autumn chill, and it would do. "That's it. It's this one, or I'm not going."

Gran squinted at the dress, a look of distaste on her face. "That's the best you can do? Why is it that everything you own makes you look like some sort of hippy school marm?"

"They do not!" I replied, crossing my arms in front of me. "I have eclectic taste. That's all."

"Eclectic taste? That's just a fancy-schmancy way to say weird. If you're ever going to catch a man, you have to do a better job of advertising the wares." Gran's hands sculpted a much more voluptuous figure in the air than mine would ever be. At five foot eight inches with short, dirty blonde hair, I don't exactly cut the most lady-like figure. Throw in the fact I have apples rather than melons (Gran's words not mine) and my jeans don't swish when I walk ("you can see daylight between those gams") and my figure is probably better described as 'boyish'.

"Advertise? Catch a man? Did you ever think that maybe I don't want a man in my life right now? I'm twenty-three, not some old maid you know." After pulling the dress on, I gave it a twirl in the mirror, liking the way the circular skirt swirled out around my knees. "I still can't believe I let you talk me into this ridiculous set up. The guy doesn't even know me. Even if we do bump into each other at the coffee shop, what makes you think we'll hit it off?"

"He doesn't know you *yet*. That's why you need to bump into him. I mean *really* bump into him. Spill your coffee on him or something. Give him a chance to get to know you. It will make a great story to tell my great-grandbabies." Gran was a big fan of the old movies where the woman and the man would meet in some cutesy manner and fall head over heels. She was determined I should have my own 'meet-cute'.

"Great-grandbabies?? Oh no, that's it. I'm not going." I collapsed on the bed, a hanger sticking me in the ribs.

"Angharad Grainne Russo, you promised me you would do it."

That's right, my name is Angharad. It's the kind of name that makes people chuckle and say 'what were your parents thinking?' I can't even blame them since my mom died bringing me into this world and my dad is a mystery she took to her grave. No, my mouthful of a moniker is all Gran's fault. And, since I know you are probably wondering, it's pronounced An-HAR-ad GRAW-nya ROO...well, I think you can get the rest. Can you blame me if I prefer to be called Harry?

"Alright, alright. One week. One week of hanging out at the coffee shop for one hour a day just to 'meet cute' your idea of Mr. Right-for-Me, then that's it."

I grabbed my navy cardigan and headed out the door. Gran didn't move fast enough and I passed through her less than corporeal body. Dead seven years and still bossing me around. Oh, that's right, I guess I hadn't mentioned that part yet. I'm like the kid in that old Bruce Willis movie. I see dead people.

***

Growing up in a community of witches, being the kid that sees ghosts, isn't exactly the strangest thing, but it's still considered pretty weird. And that's even including Meryl Doncaster whose hair used to change colour every time she sneezed, at least until she hit puberty and started to get her gift of camouflage under control.

I was the kid that knew everyone's secrets. Ghosts are terrible gossips, especially ones that know there is a medium in their midst that can pass along a message. Witches can be real bitches when they die. I didn't pass along half the things they said to me. Some things are just better left unsaid.

Gran was a very powerful hedge witch herself and although there hadn't been a medium in the community for years, she did her best to see that I learned how to control my gift. This meant that I had to learn the rituals of banishment and summons, in that order of course, it wouldn't do to summon a spirit and then not be able to get rid of it. I have never actually summoned a ghost, other than when I first learned how to do it. Ghosts just sort of find me.

I'm also pretty good with plants. I can grow just about anything, anywhere. That's why I started up my little shop, Contain Yourself, here in town, taking my green thumb to the masses, helping them grow flowers, veggies, and yes, the occasional medicinal marijuana plant, in eco-friendly containers. I actually started as an assistant when the shop was still Mrs. Potts' Flowers, but a year ago Mrs. P decided to slow down and semi-retire, so I bought the business. I wouldn't say she has slowed down much though; she still works in the shop every day. I usually just handle inventory and some of the deliveries.

Delivering flowers is a great way to put my strange gift to some use. Lots of flowers get delivered to funerals and hospitals and where there's death, there's quite often a messed up spirit wondering what the hell happened. More often than not, I just lay down the 4-1-1, point them to the proverbial light and send them on their way. Every so often though, there is something holding them back, preventing them from making the transition.

Ghosts need energy to manifest. They can do this by siphoning off the excess energy that surrounds every living thing, including the loved ones they left behind. Electrical energy can also be used, which explains why ghosts are much more prevalent now than they were a hundred years ago. Unfortunately ghosts are usually drawn to their old lives, haunting their families, drawing the energy they need to exist from the ones they love, inadvertently harming them. Grief can weigh you down, but not as much as when a spirit is sucking the life force right out of you. I do what I can to help out. I like to think of it as community service.

Which reminded me; I had a stop to make on the way to the coffee shop. With that in mind, I headed down to the shop to pick up the arrangement of flowers I had readied earlier in the day.

***

Jubilee 'just call me Juba' Daniels had lived in the same two-bedroom bungalow almost his entire life. The last twenty-five years of which he had spent with his second wife Millie. Juba was the cutest, little old man I'd ever met. Standing about 5'2" on his tip toes, he looked like a little, black Santa Claus with his big round belly and curly white beard. His beard was a real contrast with his dark, dark skin. He told me once he came from Senegal and his skin was so dark because his mother had dipped him in an inkwell to ward off evil spirits. The most memorable thing about Juba Daniels though, wasn't his dark skin or his white hair, it was his smile. You have never seen a happier, more genuine smile. It lit up his entire face from the dimple in his chin to the twinkle in his eye, and he was always smiling, especially when he talked about his wife Millie.

Every week like clockwork, Juba came into the flower shop to pick up a bouquet of cut flowers for 'his Millie'. Every week until last week that is, when instead of coming into the shop to buy flowers, he came to ask my help. Of course he was dead by that point, died in his sleep from a heart attack. Not a bad way to go I guess, except it was unexpected, like death often is, and he had a few loose ends he needed tied up.

Juba had a son from his first marriage, and as Juba put it, he was a real piece of work. Juba had tried to do his best with the boy, but his first wife had run off with a banker and took the boy with her when he was only five. After that, Juba and his son had sporadic contact and eventually the boy grew up and wanted nothing to do with his father or his father's new wife. At least not until the gentrification phenomenon hit the neighbourhood and property prices started to sky rocket. Suddenly Neville Daniels, who hadn't amounted to much (unless being a meth-head counted), became very interested in his dear old dad and specifically his dad's health.

Worried his son might try and cheat poor Millie out of her estate, Juba had gone to a lawyer and written up a will, but thinking he still had plenty of time left on this Earth, he hadn't mentioned it to Millie. That's where I came in, and from the sound of things, I was just in time.

The front door was open when I arrived at the tidy, little house. From inside I could hear a man's raised voice.

"There ain't no will old lady, that means I gets half. You pays or you get out!" The angry voice obviously meant to intimidate.

"I don't have that kind of money," Millie replied quietly. "I'm sure we can come to some sort of settlement though. Your father would have..."

"I don't give no damn what my father thought. I want my money. Don't you go holding out on me."

I stepped into the house and called out. "Hello? Mrs. Daniels? Millie? It's me, Harry."

"Who are you? What are you doing in here?" Neville came out the kitchen door and into the living room, a scowl on his face. Despite being over forty, he was dressed like a teenage 'gangsta' in baggy jeans and an oversized T-shirt. He had accessorized the winning combo with a big silver chain with a large letter 'N' dangling on it. Talk about a stereotype. "Get out of here white bitch."

"Harry, is that you?" Millie followed Neville out of the kitchen looking relieved.

I decided to ignore Neville. "It's me, Millie, and I have something for you, in honour of Juba." I held out the big bouquet of flowers I had put together. "One last bunch. I'm sorry for your loss."

"Thank you dear. I should go put them in some water." Millie took the bouquet and headed back towards the kitchen.

"I'll come with you," I replied. I started to follow Millie, brushing past Neville.

"Hey bitch. I was talking to you." He reached out and grabbed my arm. "I told you get out. I've gots some business here still."

As soon as his hand touched my arm, I stopped and reached across with my other hand to grab his thumb, flexing it back and forcing him to let go.

"Don't touch me asshole," I said, keeping my voice steady and low. I pulled his thumb back farther until he cried out. He twisted away, trying to free himself but I just followed his movement until I had his arm behind his back, his thumb pulled up at a painful angle. "Millie, maybe you should take the flowers to the kitchen."

When she was gone, I kicked out Neville's shin causing him to fall to his knees. With his arm still twisted behind his back I leaned in close and quietly said, "Listen closely. You are going to leave this house and not come back. If I hear that you have been hassling Millie, I will be back and I will be bringing the police. I'm sure they would be thrilled to speak to a tweaker like you." I pulled on Neville's arm forcing him back up to his feet and marched him to the front door where I pushed him out, releasing his thumb with a painful jerk just to get my message across. I slammed the door and locked it just as Millie returned with a vase and the flowers.

"I'm afraid your stepson had to leave," I said.

"He's not going to be happy about that. I don't know what I'm going to do."

"Don't worry Millie, Juba made sure you were taken care of."

Millie smiled sadly. "My Juba always took good care of me, but he didn't leave a will."

"But he did," I replied. "He probably just forgot to mention it to you." This was the hard part. Getting the information I needed to Millie without having to say her dead husband told me. "I remember eight months or so ago he came into the flower shop one day and he mentioned he had been to the lawyer. Are you sure he didn't leave a will somewhere in the house?"

"I don't think so. He never mentioned it to me." Millie's face looked hopeful.

"Where would Juba have hidden something important? Is there any special hiding place he might have used? Did you check there?"

"Well, I....no, I didn't think to look because I didn't know there was anything to find."

"Maybe we should look around now? I'll help."

After a few false starts, Millie finally thought to check in the old cigar box on the top shelf in the hall closet where I knew, thanks to Juba, the will would be. She was so happy she was in tears, especially when she learned she wouldn't have to move. I waited while she called the lawyer on the document and made an appointment to go see him that very afternoon. The lawyer even offered to send a car to pick her up so I felt better when it was time to leave knowing that she was in good hands. The last thing I saw before I headed off to my coffee 'date' was Jubilee Daniels sending me a little salute before he faded into the light. Not a bad day's work.

Chapter Two

The coffee shop where my supposed meet-cute was to take place, was just a couple blocks over from the old refurbished firehall that houses both me and my shop. There's a little park across the street with a clear view of the coffee shop's door. I figured that it would be a good place to park myself, grande latte in hand, to scope out the clientele. According to Gran, I was looking for a young Cary Grant, if Cary Grant was Asian. I wasn't really sure what that was either, but I wasn't going to complain about taking an hour's peace and quiet to people watch on a sunny, autumn day. At least I would have lived up to the spirit, if not the letter, of my promise to Gran to give her idea a try. I probably should have gone for the venti though, because there wasn't much left of my grande to 'accidentally' spill on Mr. Asian Cary Grant.

I had just about decided to call it a day when Mr. No-Show showed up. He really did look like an Asian Cary Grant; prominent cheekbones, high forehead, strong chin. I had to give Gran credit, she knew a hottie when she saw one. He was casually dressed in Dockers and a black v-neck t-shirt that was tight enough to show that he must make some effort at the gym. He definitely had appeal. Just my luck he was also dead.

I quickly put my head down, suddenly finding my empty coffee cup very interesting, but I knew it was too late. He'd spotted me. Or maybe he was already being drawn to me since I'm basically like a ghost magnet. When I looked up from my cup, he had disappeared from across the street and was standing beside me.

"You see me? You can see me? Oh my God! You gotta help me." The ghost made a grab for my arm, as if he wanted to pull me up from the bench, but his translucent fingers passed right though me. He looked momentarily stunned at his predicament. "Please, I need your help." He pleaded with me with his eyes.

The park was pretty busy with people coming and going, so I pulled out my cell phone and put it to my ear. It's one of the tricks of the trade when you're a medium. The last thing you want is to look like some sort of crazy person talking to thin air. I looked up at him and put on my most sympathetic face.

"Listen to me. You're dead. Go to the light," I said. I got up from the bench and threw my empty cup into the trash, ignoring the pleading spirit. What? I said I sent them on their way, not hold their hands and sing 'Kumbaya'. I'm not their grief counsellor. If there's one thing I've learned over the past few years, it's that you have to be pretty blunt when it comes to the dead. Just cut to the chase. Otherwise you'll end up getting sucked into the vortex of their self-pity. Telling it like it is usually works; unfortunately not this time.

"Please, you gotta help me. I can't go yet. There's something I have to do first." He looked at me, his desperation mirrored in his eyes. I hate it when they look at me like that. It's like looking at a puppy. It gets me every time.

"Alright, alright. What do you want me to do? Get a message to someone? Feed your cat?"

Dead Guy smiled. Wow, he could really turn on the charm. Too bad he was dead; that smile could have taken him places.

"Hurry! This way."

He evaporated only to reappear back across the street. I reluctantly followed, his spectral body blinking in and out of sight a few yards in front of me, like some sort of weird follow the bouncing ball sing along.

I found Dead Guy's body just around the corner from the coffee shop in the back lane. It looked like he had been dumped there and the killer didn't try all that hard to hide the body. I really hate looking at dead bodies. You'd think I would be used to it by now, but it doesn't get any easier. I never would have guessed the bloody, swollen bag of bones on the ground beside the dumpster could be my Asian Cary Grant. He had really taken a beating. I turned to look at the spirit beside me. "Do you remember your name?"

"My name? Of course I know my own name. I'm Bryce. Bryce Chow."

"Do you have any idea who would do this to you?"

"I...." A look of consternation passed over his handsome features. "I....I don't know. I can't remember."

No surprise there, but it was worth a shot. Generally, the memories of the recently departed are like Swiss cheese. They can usually remember their name, address and what they ate for breakfast, but the minutes leading up to their death? Gone like a prom queen's virginity in the back of a Chevy. Looking at what had once been Bryce Chow, I guess it's a mercy.

"I really can't remember. Why can't I remember?" Bryce moaned.

"It's just the way it is. Listen Bryce, you've got to focus. Why did you need me to come here? What is it that you still have to do?"

"I....the stick. The memory stick. They didn't find it." He clutched at his ghostly head as if he could yank the memories out. "Why can't I remember who *they* are?"

"I don't know. I'll do what I can to help you find out. Where do I find this memory stick?"

"It's in my shoe, my left shoe."

"Crap! I don't want to touch you." I made a face of disgust. "Didn't you ever watch TV? I'll leave fingerprints or trace evidence or something."

"Come on girl, you've got to help me."

A quick look around the back lane revealed that the only security camera in range appeared to be broken. Luckily, the shoe in question wasn't as dirty as the other and I was able to grasp it with my hands in the sleeves of my sweater. The heel swiveled open with a little persuasion and inside I found a USB memory stick. I pocketed the stick, closed the secret compartment back up and then got the hell out of there.

At the entrance to the lane I stopped and pulled out my cell phone.

"What are you doing?" Bryce's incorporeal self was beginning to become more translucent. I was surprised he lasted as long as he did. As I said, manifesting as a ghost requires energy. Usually the newbies don't have much juice and their appearances are fleeting at best.

"I have to call the cops. If I don't, and someone saw me enter the alley, they'll wonder why I didn't call it in. Trust me. It's the right thing to do."

Chapter Three

Trust me...Famous last words. Why is it that the right thing to do isn't necessarily the best thing? After waiting twenty minutes for a squad car to show up, the uniforms had left me to cool my heels on the same park bench I had occupied before. This wasn't my first rodeo or even my second for that matter, when it came to finding a dead body. I knew they would keep me waiting for the detectives assigned to the case to arrive. This time though, there seemed to be some confusion because the first suits that showed up just waited around for another car to arrive. The four men had a little confab then the first two, looking a little disgruntled, hopped back in their car and took off. The whole scene smacked of office politics. Somebody had pulled some strings to get the second pair of detectives assigned to the case. What had Bryce gotten himself into? I'd have asked him, but he had long since dissipated.

The second set of detectives looked less than pleased to be called in. They both looked a little bleary eyed, like they had just woken up, but since it was now after three in the afternoon, that didn't seem likely, unless they were on the night shift or something. The pair made an odd couple. One was a short, slim, mixed race-African American with warm mocha skin and short dreadlocks. His sharp, charcoal grey suit complete with tie seemed completely antithetical to the dreads. The second of the pair towered over his partner. He had to be at least six foot four and had the well-proportioned build of someone who works out and not just to build upper body bulk for show. He was also wearing a shirt and tie, but had gone for a more casual look, wearing a black leather jacket instead of a suit, and Dockers that hugged his ass nicely. His short, light brown hair had that tousled, just got out of bed look that made you want to run your fingers through it.

"You're staring at Nash and licking your lips."

"Bryce!" His voice in my ear practically startled me right off the bench. "I was not."

"You were too."

He materialized on the bench beside me. I cast a furtive look over to the uniform supposedly babysitting me, but he didn't appear to have noticed my outburst. "I was not.....hey, wait a minute. Whose ass? You know that guy?"

"Of course I do. Everyone does."

"Well, obviously not everyone. I don't know him or his partner."

"The partner is Dev, Devlin Mayes. How can you be part of the Cimmerian and not know Nash and Dev?"

"The Cimmerian! I'm not a criminal. I don't associate with them." The Cimmerian was the collective name for the darker side of the supernatural community, a community that for the most part, remained in the closet. Taken from Greek mythology it meant dwellers of the dark and gloom. That Bryce knew the name for the local criminal underworld, spoke volumes as to why he ended up beaten into a bloody pulp. "How were you associated to them?" I looked at him suspiciously. "You weren't a Cutter were you?"

"A vamp-wannabe? No way, I try to steer clear of bloodsuckers."

Vampires made up the majority of the Cimmerian society and had a hierarchical power structure. Cutters, basically humans that longed to be vampires were the

15

lowest in the pecking order, the lackeys and sycophants of the true vampires. They took their name from their unnatural habit of sucking each other's blood. Since they didn't have fangs, they used razor blades to slice their skin. Occasionally, a Cutter who ingratiated himself to a particularly powerful vampire, a 'Vlad', would be granted the right to be turned, which of course gave all the other Cutters hope of immortality and brought more of the Goth freaks to the service of the vampires.

"If you steer clear of vampires how do you even know about the Cimmerian then?"

"I said I *tried* to steer clear of them, but I do work for them or at least I did. I was a computer security consultant for the Magister."

Salvador Arroyo, the Magister. Based on the company he kept, it really came as no surprise that Bryce ended up a bloody smudge in a back lane. The Kingpin of the underworld, Salvador Arroyo was the most powerful Vlad in Riverton and as the Magister for the Cimmerian it made him the leader of the entire supernatural community. Arroyo owned a multinational corporation and had his fingers in a lot of pies, mostly those that involved sex, drugs and alcohol. Gambling was another of his cornerstone industries. It wasn't much of a stretch of the imagination to figure he might own a few corrupt cops as well.

"And how do Detective Nash and his partner come into play?" I asked Bryce, but he had disappeared again.

I looked over to the mouth of the alley only to see Nash and his partner staring at me. Just great, they probably saw me talking to myself. I made a show of getting up from the bench and gathering up my things.

16

When I turned around, Detective Nash was standing beside me. I looked up into his eyes and, this is going to sound totally cliché and corny, but time stood still. Seriously. It was like everything ceased to exist except his startling green eyes. My heart thumped in my chest. For a moment, he had a look of complete shock on his face and then he inhaled and a frown replaced the shock and time started to move again. I let out the breath I didn't know I had been holding.

"Detective Nash." I held out my hand for him to shake. "Harry Russo. Nice to meet you, well, I mean it's not nice under the circumstances but..." Damn, I was totally babbling. "I...can I go now? I gave my statement to the officer and I really have nothing more to add."

"You're Harry Russo?" Detective Nash shook my hand and held onto it. "Harry? Really?"

"Yes, that's me. It's a nickname." I tried to pull my hand back but it was held fast. "Could I, um, have my hand back?"

"Your hand?" He looked at me in confusion then looked down to see our hands still clasped together. "Of course. Sorry. It was the name. You're not what I expected."

He released my hand and I pulled it back and held it protectively against my chest. My whole hand tingled from his touch.

"No problem. I get that all the time. Kind of goes with the territory when you're a girl named Harry."

"Yes, I guess it does." He gestured to his partner. "This is Detective Mayes. We just have a few questions for you."

"Yes of course. But I really don't know what I could add to the statement I already made."

"It won't take long. Would you like to sit down?"

"No thanks. I've been warming that bench for almost two hours now. I'd really just like to get back to work. They'll be wondering what happened to me."

"Yes, I see. So you didn't call them to let them know you were being detained?"

"No. The officer said I shouldn't make any calls."

"Then who were you talking to just now?"

"Talking to? I wasn't talking to anyone."

"But we just saw you talking to someone a minute ago."

"Oh that." I smiled self-consciously. "I wasn't talking to anyone. I was just making some notes on my phone. Gotta love voice recognition." I pulled my cell phone out of my purse and gave it a little shake. "Can't live without it these days."

"Right. May I see?" He held his hand out for my phone which I reluctantly gave him. He pressed a key and the screen lock came on.

"Oh, you just..." I swiped my finger over the screen and then punched in the lock code. The home screen flashed on with a picture of me and my two roommates posing like *Charlie's Angels*.

He selected the call log and saw that there were no incoming or outgoing calls in the last two hours then thumbed the button to take him back to the home screen.

"And these two others are?" He gestured to the picture.

"Those are my roommates, Holly and Tess. We're posing like *Charlie's Angels*. You know...like...." I struck a pose, fake finger gun held up in front of me.

"Uh-huh. So, how did you know the deceased?"

"I didn't. I mean I don't."

"And why were you in the alley?"

Luckily, I had prepared myself for that question. "I was going to look in the recycling for boxes I could reuse." It was something I did quite often, although never here at the coffee shop.

"So start from the beginning and tell us everything you saw."

"Do I really need to go over everything again?"

"Yes."

I sat back down on the bench. This was going to take a while; might as well get comfortable.

Chapter Four

"Gran!" I dumped my purse on the kitchen island and went straight for the cupboard. "Gran?" Of course she was a no show. What a disaster her little set up turned out to be. The entire afternoon spent being grilled by the police and I still had the headache of figuring out what Bryce needed me to do for him.

My roommates, Tess and Holly, were both still at work. Tess worked at her uncle's gym and Holly worked as a nurse at the nearby Riverton Hospital. The three of us lived above my shop on the second and third floors of the firehall. A deal with the building's owner had allowed us to sink some money into the place, with the understanding that we would be able to buy the building from him in five more years' time when he retired and moved back home to India. The second floor was shared space with an open concept living room and kitchen. There was also some storage, a powder room, and the laundry on this floor. We converted the third floor dormitories into three spacious bedrooms each complete with its own ensuite. The best part was the roof top greenhouse and garden. The building's flat style roof had allowed me to create a green oasis in the city. Besides a kitchen herb and vegetable garden, I cultivated many of the plants and flowers there that ended up in customer containers for the shop.

Since I was alone and didn't feel like making anything to eat, I grabbed a jar of peanut butter, a bottle of chocolate syrup and a spoon from the cupboard, sat down on one of the stools at the kitchen island and dug a big spoonful of peanut butter out of the jar. Next I drizzled on some chocolate sauce then stuck the whole spoonful in my mouth. Hey, don't knock it 'til you've tried it. I was seriously running low on energy reserves. Communicating with cops and ghosts will do that to you. Okay, so the cops were just really frustrating. It's ghosts that are draining. One of the pitfalls of being a medium; ghosts have to get the energy to manifest from somewhere and a medium is like having a telephone and a battery rolled into one handy package. When I started to feel drained like this, the best thing for it was carbs followed by a protein chaser, thus the peanut butter and chocolate sauce. Not to mention it tasted damn good too.

I poured myself a big glass of milk and then pulled the memory stick out of my pocket to look at it. It was just a standard USB memory stick. What could be on it that was worth killing for? I guess there was only one way to find out. After firing up the old computer sitting in the corner of the living room, I inserted the memory stick and opened it up. There was only one file on the stick, a rather large video file. Great, it was starting to look like Bryce was killed for a sex tape.

Knowing I would probably regret it, I clicked on the icon to play the video, but instead of getting someone's naughty home movie, a security screen popped open asking for a password.

"You need the RSA token."

"Bryce! Quit doing that." My heart pounded in my chest. You'd think I would be used to voices coming out of nowhere by now. "What's an RSA token? Do you know what's on this video?"

Bryce took form behind me, looking over my shoulder at the monitor and frowning. "No, I can't remember. I just know it's something important,

21

something very important and I want to trade it for Bianca, my sister."

"Your sister? You mean she's being held for ransom or something?"

"No, no, nothing like that."

It turned out Bryce's younger sister had a bit of a gambling problem. She had dug herself into a hole so deep that even her brother couldn't help dig her out by legitimate means. That's why Bryce had started working for Salvador Arroyo in the first place, to work off her debt by doing some less than legal computer security.

"And now that I'm, uh, well dead, I need to get her out of debt once and for all."

"Well without the password we don't even know what's on here and if it is even worth trading. How do we find the password to look at it?"

"You need to get the RSA token and use it to enter a code. I have one at my place. I must have copied the video from somewhere and used the token to protect it."

"Can't you just hack the password?"

"No, it's 128-bit encryption. I can't hack it. You just need to go to my place and get the token then we can use it to unlock the file."

"Go to your place? Are you kidding? I'm sure the cops are all over it. I can't just waltz in there. What if someone sees me?"

"I can get you in so you won't be seen. There's a fire escape around the back and the bedroom window doesn't lock properly. The sooner you find out what's on that video, the sooner you can get rid of me."

Solving Bryce's problem and sending him on his way was high on my list of things to do, even if I did have to do a little break and entering. "Okay, okay. But I need to stop for a burger on the way."

***

The third storey window to Bryce's apartment was unlocked, just like he said it would be. What he neglected to mention was that the fire escape ended at the living room window and that I would have to shimmy along a narrow ledge to get to the bedroom. I had grilled Bryce as much as I could about where to look for the token in his apartment before I had left because it was more than likely that he would be a no show when I needed him. You can't really predict when or if a spirit will manifest, at least not without performing some sort of summoning ritual.

Rather than lingering on the ledge and risk someone seeing me, I quickly climbed through the window, but then stayed crouched beside the bed so I could scope things out. The bedroom door was open and I could see straight into the living room. Either Bryce was a complete slob, or someone had already tossed the place. It was going to be next to impossible to find anything in the chaos that once had been Bryce's stuff. Still, I crept into the living room to see if luck was maybe on my side.

Bryce said he used a laptop but, of course, there was no sign of one. Either the cops or the people that killed him had beat me to it. It didn't matter; I wasn't looking for his computer. I was looking for a small keychain fob with a digital display. Like that would be easier to find.

I started at the most obvious place, the desk. It had been ransacked; the drawers pulled out and dumped on the floor. Beside it, the bookshelf and all the books it once held had been equally turned out. The heathens had even ripped apart some of the books looking for whatever might be hidden in the spines or covers. At least most of the casualties seemed to be computer textbooks.

The kitchen and the dining room were also a bust. The last place to look was the living room. Bryce said he more often sat on the sofa than at his desk when working. Unfortunately, it had fared worse than the books. The cushions were strewn about the room and someone had taken a knife to them, the stuffing torn and spilling out, the back of the frame cut to ribbons. Feeling defeated, I flopped down on the bare sofa frame to think.

Remarkably, the end table still stood beside the sofa, although the lamp that used to sit on it lay smashed on the floor. I tried to imagine Bryce working there. He probably would have set the token on the end table but a search of the floor around it turned up nothing, not even the remote, but since the TV was also missing, I guess that was no surprise. It looked like Bryce's killers helped themselves to his 50" LCD TV as well as his life.

I was beginning to think this little field trip was a total waste of time. It was a shame about Bryce's nice leather couch, although I guess he wouldn't need it anymore. I ran my hand along the soft leather, smooth as butter. I guess that's what gave me my sudden epiphany, thinking about butter melting and sliding down the sculpted sofa arms. When you are sitting on your sofa where does everything end up? I slid my hand along the soft leather arm until I reached the point where it met the seat. You know what I'm talking about; the place where all the loose change and food crumbs go. I tried not to think about what all might be down there, when my fingers brushed against something hard and plastic. Bingo!

Clutching the token, I headed back to the bedroom just as I heard a key turning in the lock. I dove under the bed as the apartment door opened.

"Damn! They sure did a number on this place."

"Doesn't look like we'll get much help here," a familiar voice replied.

Detective Nash! Just my luck he would show up now. I huddled under the bed and held my breath. Nash and his partner, Dev, walked through the living room, randomly looking at the mess. When he reached the sofa, Nash stopped and inhaled deeply, a puzzled look on his face. He had done the same thing several times when I spoke with him earlier. He must have a sinus problem or something.

My heart started to pound so loudly I was sure they would hear it. I took a few slow breaths and focused on lowering my heart rate, a skill Gran drilled into me when I was younger. When Nash reached the bedroom, I figured my goose was cooked. Luckily, I had thought to close the window behind me when I had entered the apartment. Nash stood beside the bed and examined the window, discovering the broken lock. He inhaled deeply again and his feet, clad in well-worn, black motorcycle boots, came to the side of the bed.

"Hey man, this is getting us nowhere. Let's get out of here." Dev called from the living room.

"Yeah, I guess you're right. Anything that might have led to the killers is long gone," Nash replied as he walked back towards the living room.

I lay under the bed for at least another five minutes after they left. That had been too close for comfort. It was getting dark by that point and rather than use the window, I decided to risk using the door. I really didn't want to climb out on that ledge again.

Chapter Five

"You did what?"

"Without me?"

Both Holly and Tess were home when I arrived with my prize and a bit of an adrenaline buzz from the whole adventure. Their polar opposite responses after I gave them the *Reader's Digest* version of what had happened, pretty much summed up their personalities.

Always my partner in crime, Tess and I had been raised together having both lost our parents as young kids - I never knew mine and Tess's parents were killed in a car accident when she was a toddler. In typical Tess fashion, she was a bit miffed I committed a break and enter without her. Short and scrappy with a gorgeous head of shoulder length, wavy, black hair and Latino features, she's a real knock-out who can literally knock you out with one punch. Trained in a multitude of martial arts, from Tai Chi to Krav Maga, she has black belts in four of them and beats up men twice her size on a daily basis at her uncle's gym. She can also bench press twice her body weight, of course the fact that she's a werewolf may have something to do with that.

Holly, on the other hand, is a curvy blonde who looks like she belongs on the set of a California surfer movie. Her golden locks and perpetual tan, courtesy of no small talent in magical body modification, accentuate her usually sunny disposition (although she looked pretty stormy right now). Being five years older than us, Holly was often the *de facto* babysitter when we were growing up and when Gran died seven years ago and I was still under age, she stepped in. Caring was just in Holly's nature; I didn't think she could turn it off if she tried. It was probably a side effect of being a hearth witch with a very strong gift in healing. You end up getting a full dose of empathy to go with it.

"I can't believe that guy your Gran wanted to set you up with is dead." Tess flopped down on the sofa. "Was he at least good looking?"

"Really Tess," Holly scolded sternly, "a man is dead. It shouldn't matter what he looked like."

I looked around for any sign of Bryce but the coast was clear. "Holly's right, but yeah, he was pretty hot." I fired up the old computer again and stuck the USB memory stick back in. "Let's hope this works so I can help him out."

"You should really just throw that in the trash." Holly shook her finger at me. "You shouldn't get any more involved than you already are."

"That's the whole point. I'm already involved. I can't ignore it now and I'm not throwing it out or turning it over to anyone until I know what it is," I replied.

I clicked on the video and the password prompt appeared again. I entered Bryce's four digit PIN then the six digit number currently displayed on the RSA Token. This time the video started to play. The picture was kind of grainy because of low lighting, but you could still make things out. It appeared to be a security feed from an empty warehouse or parking garage. There was a small group of people in the background of the frame. At first you couldn't really see them, but then the camera began to zoom in bringing them to the foreground.

"I don't like the look of this," I said, shaking my head slowly. The small group appeared to be two men standing over a third man on his knees on the floor. His hands were bound behind his back and he was wearing a blind fold. There appeared to be several people in the shadows watching. I clicked pause on the video. "Uh... guys...you better come look at this."

Holly and Tess both came over to stand behind me and I started the video back up. The two men that were standing grasped a long knife together and held it aloft. They appeared to be chanting but there was no audio with the video so we couldn't hear what they were saying. The kneeling man began to struggle until one of the standing men grabbed his hair, pulling the man's head back. He yanked off the blindfold.

"They're not going to..." Tess leaned in closer to get a better look.

"I think they are," I replied in shock.

"I can't watch." Holly turned away from the monitor.

The men holding the knife suddenly plunged it into the chest of the kneeling man. He crumpled to the floor and one of the other men held the knife aloft again. The man holding the knife continued to chant for a moment then appeared to wipe his thumb along the blood on the blade. He turned to his fellow murderer and drew a symbol on his forehead. For a minute nothing happened, then the man with the symbol began to convulse. Two other men rushed from the shadows and grabbed him as he began to fall to the floor, laying him down carefully. The man with the knife turned back to the body of the murdered man and cut his bonds, taking some blood from the knife and wiping it on the dead man's lips. He bent over the corpse with the bloody lips.

"Eww, he's going to kiss the dead guy!" Tess made a disgusted face.

Holly turned back, unable to look away any longer. "It looks like he's doing CPR."

"I don't get it," I said. "Why kill a guy only to then try and save him?" The whole thing was messed up. I had never seen anything like it.

"This can't be real. The whole video must be a fake." Holly began to pace. "You should just throw it away and we'll forget we ever saw it."

"Wait," Tess pointed to the screen. "What the hell is happening now?"

The guy with the knife was standing again, watching as the formerly dead guy jumped to his feet. The dead guy pumped his fists in the air. If there had been sound, I'm sure we would have heard him roar in triumph.

"Did they just do what I think they did?" I looked from Tess to Holly. Their faces both held the same disbelief that I'm sure mine did. The men on the video had just jacked the dead guy's body.

Chapter Six

There are a lot of scary things that go bump in the night that norms, what we call you non-magical folk, prefer to think are just stories. Vampires, witches, werewolves – they all exist – along with a myriad of other fantastical supernatural beings. Basically, if it's made its way into literature, you can bet there is an actual kernel of truth from which the tale sprouted. Most non-humans prefer to keep their interactions with norms to a minimum but there are some that deal with humans, even *need* humans for their existence. The Cimmerian was what resulted from that need, providing an avenue for human-supernatural interaction, some would even say exploiting it, while ensuring that for the most part, the shadow world stays just that, in the shadows.

The one story that norms manage to get wrong more often than not is the zombie. Zombies are not the shambling, brain sucking monsters you see in *Night of the Living Dead*, at least they aren't when they're done right. When called from the grave by a skilled and powerful practitioner, a zombie looks almost alive. They can walk, run, talk to some extent, but most importantly, they have superhuman strength. They aren't indestructible, but because they are magically animated and feel no pain, they can take a lot of damage before they stop. The good thing about zombies is that they can only be made by someone with the extremely rare gift of necromancy. A gift so rare, it has been generations since the last one was recorded.

As with anything though, there is always someone looking for an easier way. These are usually low level sorcerers that resort to blood magic to try and create a zombie. Jacks are one of the most heinous of these attempts and until now, I thought they were just a story.

As we saw on the video, to create a jack, the sorcerer has to use the magical energy released by a violent death to reanimate the body with the spirit of another, usually someone who is really good at astral projection. Basically, the second sorcerer, the guy we saw convulse on the video, is spirit walking using the dead guy's body. He's hijacked it.

"I didn't think that was really possible." Tess shook her head and looked at me. "Is it?"

"I've only read about it. I didn't think it had ever been done either."

"It's not possible," Holly replied adamantly. "This whole thing must be some sort of scam."

"I don't know, it looked pretty real to me. But how did they do it?"

"No, not how," answered Tess, "but why?"

***

After much back and forth, we finally gave up trying to figure out the how and the why, and came up with a plan. Tess and I felt we had to tell somebody about the video. Holly thought we should just forget the whole thing but was outnumbered. Obviously, we couldn't take it to the police. We would have to go to the Cimmerian and the Magister. After all, it was his bailiwick so to speak. But, since the video belonged to Bryce and he more than likely died trying to get it to the Magister himself, I felt we owed it to him to figure out a way to use it to get his sister out of debt as well. Not to mention, it would cut the last ties holding him here and he could go on his ghostly way.

"This whole thing is a mistake. But if you insist on going, I should go with you." Holly looked at us worriedly.

"No, for the last time, it's too dangerous for you to go." Tess shook her head.

The only way to get to the Magister was to go to one of his clubs downtown. The aptly named Dante's Inferno, was a multi-leveled nightclub that catered to the Cimmerian, mostly vamps and their human entourage, but shifters and werewolves like Tess were also welcome. Werewolves are pretty pack oriented though, tending to keep to Wolf-only bars and most don't associate with vamps if they can help it. Holly had never been part of the Cimmerian, managing to fly under the radar and keep her gifts hidden. We didn't want to change that by bringing her to the attention of the most powerful baddie in town.

"Well, if it's too dangerous for me, it's too dangerous for Harry."

"I have to go. I'm the one making the deal. Besides, I'm not completely defenceless." Like Tess, I also spent time under her uncle's tutelage, mainly learning Kali, a martial arts style that focused on the ability to fight both with a weapon or empty handed and where the goal was to inflict serious, if not lethal, damage to your opponent as quickly as possible. I was also taking along a little extra protection in the form of my katana, a weapon I had been training with at Gran's insistence since the age of twelve.

"They're never going to let you in wearing that thing." Holly gestured to the blade.

"Sure they will. They won't even notice it." I slid the katana into its sheath and adjusted its harness across my back. I liked to wear it across my back with the handle just to the right, behind my head. It made for the fastest access, allowing me to already have it in motion in a downward defensive sweep the moment it cleared the sheath. The black strap of the harness crossed my chest, but for the most part blended in with the black leather bustier I donned for the occasion. Of course, the little 'no-see-me' spell I had cast on it, would also help.

Both Tess and I had changed into clothes suitable to mix with the crowd at Dante's, which meant we were both wearing a lot of black and showing a lot of skin. Luckily, the three of us had all dressed up as biker chicks last year for Halloween so finding something to wear wasn't a problem.

Up top, I had on the short leather bustier that left my midriff bare and gave me the appearance of more cleavage than I actually had. Down below, I was wearing the equivalent of daisy dukes in black leather over top of some lacy, fishnet stockings. I finished off the ensemble with a pair of black, knee-height, lace up Doc Martens and a silver-spiked dog collar. The collar sounds over-the-top, but it wasn't. It was actually the most important piece I wore besides my katana. The spikes were real silver and the collar itself would indicate to the vamp population that I wasn't on the menu. I pulled on a black leather jacket to ward off the chill and to cover my bare shoulders and arms. I looked totally badass or hilarious, depending on whom you asked.

Tess was similarly dressed, but showing a great deal more bare skin. With her werewolf metabolism she wouldn't feel the cold and besides, she was supposed to be the distraction so that I could go unnoticed.

Chapter Seven

It was just after midnight when we arrived at Dante's and as expected, the party was just getting started, the line was only half a block long rather than the full block it would be later. It didn't matter, we weren't planning on waiting in line.

As I had hoped, the bouncer at the door was a low-level vampire. He looked like something out of a Goth nightmare. Actually, he looked a lot like Ozzy Osborne, round, purple lensed glasses and all, so it was a surprise when the words out of his mouth sounded straight out of Jersey rather than jolly old England.

"Hey! Youse gals will have to get back in line."

"We're here to see Mr. Arroyo. I have an appointment." I tried to keep on my best poker face.

Bouncer Ozzy just laughed. "Yeah, youse and all these udders."

I stepped up closer to him and made eye contact. His pupils widened in surprise. Usually people try to avoid direct eye contact with a vamp no matter how low level.

"You need to let us through. I have an appointment."

"Uh, yeah. I need to let youse through. You have an appointment." He reached over and unhooked the velvet rope that blocked the entrance. The crowd in line started to complain. Tess shot them a cheeky grin.

"So long suckers," she said.

"Tess!" I grabbed her arm and pulled her through the door. "Don't tease the animals. We're trying not to be noticed, remember?"

"Okay, okay, but that was nuts. It was so 'these aren't the droids you're looking for'."

"What?"

"You know, from *Star Wars*? Obi-wan?"

"I know what you're talking about. I've only watched it a bazillion times with you. But I don't see what it has to do with right now."

"You don't think it was a little strange that the bouncer back there just let us in?"

Yes, as a matter of fact, I did. As for the reason why it worked, that was something I preferred to leave in Egypt, you know, the land of denial.

I was saved from replying when we came to the end of the long, dark hallway leading into the club. As we stepped through the door our senses were assaulted. The music was hearing-loss inducing loud; some sort of thrash metal, Slayer or Metallica maybe. The main floor of the club was a seething mass of bodies. It was hard to really see anything except glimpses because of the low lighting and the strobe effect lights flashing on and off all over the dance floor. It was enough to send an epileptic into seizure.

Across the wide expanse of the main floor there was a curved staircase that led up to a second level balcony. It provided a more intimate setting with lots of dark corners where the cutters and the blood whores could indulge in their addictions while low level vamps trolled for their next meal.

The atmosphere of the club was wired. I could feel the energy pulsing around the room. It was a heady experience and for a moment my knees buckled as I soaked it all in.

"Hey. Are you okay?" Tess looked at me with concern and grabbed my arm to steady me.

"Yeah, yeah. I'm fine." I took a deep breath. "Can't you feel it?"

"Feel what?"

"It feels so alive. Like the whole place has a pulse."

Tess frowned and dragged me away from the door towards a stand up table against the wall. "Get a grip on yourself. We don't need you getting all high right now. Are you sure you can do this?"

"I'm fine, I'm fine." I shook off her concern. "It just took me by surprise, that's all. I've got it under control now."

The waitress came by and we ordered a couple of beers while we scoped out the place.

"That's where you need to go, there." Tess pointed to a wall of windows over the dance floor. "It's the Magister's private lounge."

"Yeah, but how do I get up there?" Frowning, I searched the perimeter of the room closest to the windows. There had to be a staircase or something. After a few minutes, my scrutiny was rewarded. A door opened in the side of the wall and two large, gorilla-like men came down a hidden staircase and then stood on either side of the open door. They looked like Tweedle-dee and Tweedle-dum on steroids, almost identical twins in dark suits with dark coloured shirts and ties. They were all upper-body strength, bulging necks and biceps, with narrow waists.

Tess had noticed them as well. "Great. How are we going to get past the goon squad over there?" I had been wondering that myself. They weren't vamps but they probably weren't completely human either.

"I think the direct method is the best approach." I downed the rest of my beer then set off across the room.

"Hey! Wait up! What are you going to do?" Tess hurried after me.

"Trust me. I've got a plan."

Tweedle-one and his brother, Tweedle-two, had been watching me since about halfway across the room. You had to give them credit, as security they knew what they were doing. While I doubt if I appeared as a threat, they quickly discerned that I was going to be something they needed to deal with momentarily.

As I approached, the closest goon put up a hand to stop me.

"This is a private entrance."

"I need to see Mr. Arroyo." I tried to sound as business-like as anyone could while yelling over top of Metallica's *Thunderstruck*.

"Mr. Arroyo doesn't see anyone without an appointment." Tweedle-one dismissed me by turning his gaze back towards the dance floor.

"Oh, he'll want to see me. Just tell him I have a message from Bryce Chow, a very important message."

"And why would I want to do that? What's in it for me?" He leered at me, making it obvious what he thought he should get.

"How about your life, asshole." Tess glared at him. I gave her a quick elbow. Antagonizing the gorilla wasn't going to help.

"Yes, your life." I looked at him appraisingly. "I imagine that's probably what you will lose when Mr. Arroyo finds out you turned us away and he didn't get the information we have for him."

The two Tweedles shifted uncomfortably. That had got their attention. They had a little *tête-à-tête* then Tweedle-two went up the stairs, leaving the first guy to give us the stink eye.

"I'm going to enjoy kicking you two sweethearts to the curb." He punched his fist into his hand menacingly. How cliché.

"You can try." Tess made her own fist. I pushed her back to a table along the wall.

"Will you put a sock in it? Geez, I can't take you anywhere." And she was the one supposed to be keeping *me* out of trouble. No surprise really. Tess was like a Chihuahua when challenged, all hackles on end and a mouthful of teeth ready to snap your finger off. Major *faux pas*, I know, to compare a werewolf to a dog, they absolutely hated that, but the description was apt.

Tweedle-two arrived back downstairs and whispered something to his partner. From the look on Tweedle-one's face, I knew we were getting in to see the Magister. I tried to keep from looking too smug as I approached the door.

As I passed by and started up the stairs, Tweedle-one stuck out his arm to stop Tess. "Just her." He hitched his thumb to point at me then looked back at Tess with a smile. "You stay."

"What? No way." Tess pushed his arm away, but the two men just moved to block the door, arms folded across their bulging chests.

"It's okay Tess. Wait here and watch the door. Make sure no surprises follow me up." Brave words, when I really didn't know what awaited me upstairs. I turned and started up before she could protest, hoping she knew better than to start trouble with the Tweedle brothers.

The narrow staircase had a little jog about three quarters of the way up. When you came out at the top, you were at the back of the room but facing the wall of windows. The stairs came right up out of the floor with a little half wall on either side to keep anyone from falling down and breaking their neck. The room was plush, done up with shades of burgundy and charcoal, with a thick, deep pile carpet and upholstered seating around the periphery. In the centre of the room, closer to the front near the windows, a large u-shaped leather sectional faced out to look over the dance floor below. It was occupied by several people and despite never having seen him before, I knew the Magister the moment I saw him. How could anyone not notice the sheer power that came off him in waves? He was of average build, appearing to be in his mid to late thirties, of course you probably had to multiply that number by at least twenty to come anywhere close to his real age. He was clean shaven with short brown hair, a hawkish nose, and a distinctly Mediterranean complexion. He was flanked on either side by a scantily-clad woman, both human arm-candy if ever I saw it, with barely enough fabric between the two of them to make even one dress.

At one end of the sectional sat a tall, brooding man who looked like he fell straight out of the pages of *GQ*; his dark hair slicked back, his lean frame clad in what was probably a bespoke designer suit. The weird sixth sense I have that helps me distinguish between low-level vamps and other more dangerous ones, was off kilter when I looked at him. He read as a powerful vampire, but seemed to be human. Whatever the case, I definitely felt a danger vibe when I looked at Mr. GQ. He must have sensed my stare, because he looked over at me in disdain before returning his gaze to his drink and the dance floor below.

A thin, slightly greasy looking vamp, dressed like an undertaker in an off the rack, three piece suit, stood guard at the top of the stairs.

"Well, well, what do we have here? Someone sent up dessert."

He sniggered at his own joke and looked over to a nearby table where a couple of his cronies joined in. He reached out with his hand as if to caress my face.

"Don't touch me." The words came out a little more forcefully than I had intended. A hush came over the room and suddenly we were the centre of attention. I concentrated on keeping my breathing regular and my heart from racing, silently thanking Gran for making me learn just how to do it. "I'm here to see the Magister. He's expecting me." The words came out steadier than I would have thought.

The vamp pulled his hand back as if burned and took a step back. Across the room, Mr. GQ rose from his seat. I was beginning to think that this plan was a very bad idea; okay, I already knew that, but it looked like it was time to make a hasty retreat and cut my losses. I was just about to turn and make a run for it back down the stairs when a gravelly voice, oozing with seduction said, "Don't be afraid, little one. Come closer."

There were close to a dozen other people, human and vampire, in the room, but I knew the comment was directed at me. It was like his voice had whispered directly in my ear. A chill ran down my spine and I shivered.

He pushed the closest bimbo from his lap. "Girls, go powder your noses or something." The two bimbos in question rose, one with a little moue of distaste on her face, and left the room through a door at the back that I hadn't noticed before.

"Come, come. You wished to see me and now you can. Come forward. Don't be shy." His voice was husky, like a smoker's and still carried a hint of his Spanish descent, but it had a pull like a siren call.

Too late to back out now, I had no choice but to move forward. I took a tentative step, all eyes still on me, then another. I scanned the room. Mr. GQ, still standing on the opposite side of the sofa, stared at me, the contempt plain on his face. I was obviously something beneath him and it was an affront that I should be here in his presence. Or maybe it was that I dared to stand before the Magister? Whatever the case, his disdain only made me more determined. I took a deep breath then strode with more confidence than I felt to stand not in front, but just off to the side, opposite from Mr. GQ.

Now what? Was I supposed to bow or something? GQ stared at me menacingly. The Magister laughed. "My dear Tomas. Sit, sit. You're going to scare our little mouse with that look of yours." He gestured for Mr. GQ, a.k.a. Tomas, to sit down.

Tomas reluctantly sat back down at his end of the sectional and grabbed his drink. I took that as my cue to speak.

"I... I'm sorry for disturbing you." I paused, what the hell was I supposed to call him? Your Majesty? "Mr. Arroyo. My name is – "

A noise at the stairs drew our attention. The greasy guard came forward. "Excuse me Magister, but Detective Nash is here to see you."

Unbelievable! The guy was like a bad penny, always turning up where he wasn't wanted. Was he following me or something? The last thing I needed was to have him here when I showed the Magister the piece

43

of evidence I withheld from the police. Not to mention the whole break and enter thing.

"Ahh, Detective Nash, my friend. Come, come. We were just about to meet this lovely, young lady." He made a come forward gesture with his hand. Nash strode into the room and glared angrily at me before looking at the Magister.

"Salvador, Tomas." Nash nodded at the two men on the sofa. "Sorry to barge in like this." He stepped closer and grabbed me by the elbow. "You'll have to excuse us but we have some police business to discuss."

The vehemence in his voice took me by surprise and I yanked my arm from his grasp, taking a step away from him.

"Nonsense," the Magister purred. "I do believe the young lady, what did you say your name was again my dear?"

"Harry, Harry Russo," I stammered it out.

"Harry?" A little smile crossed his face. "How intriguing." He turned back to Nash. "I'm afraid your business will just have to wait, my friend. The lovely Miss Harry Russo needs a moment of my time and she was here first." He smiled again but it was the smile of the cat that caught the canary - and was about to eat it.

He gestured to the seat beside him. "Come! Sit! Have a drink." He snapped his fingers and a man dressed as a waiter appeared from the shadows. "Fetch Detective Nash a glass of the 1608 he enjoys so much."

"This isn't a social call," Nash replied as he glared at me again.

"Oh, but I insist." The words slid from his mouth like butter, the compelling force behind them palpable, but still Salvador smiled like we were all friends.

Knowing he was backed into a corner, Nash gave me one last glare before letting himself drop down on the end of the sofa opposite of Tomas. The waiter appeared with Nash's drink and he tossed the expensive blended Irish whiskey back in one swallow.

Salvador smiled at me. "Now Miss Russo, do join us." He patted the seat beside him. I looked from him to Nash and then back again. There was no way I was sitting down between those two.

"I'd prefer to stand if you don't mind."

Salvador shrugged. "Lady's choice." He sat back, he eyes travelling over my body. I may have been dressed for the rabble downstairs, but up here, I felt seriously out of place. Nash seemed to take a good look at me for the first time as well, his eyes widening in surprise.

I tried to ignore the growing sensation of unease, but when the small hairs on my arms began to stand on end and my skin began to tingle, I slammed my personal shields on to full force. While low-level vampires are much like the ones found in stories, sucking blood using retractable fangs, a few, very powerful vampires achieve the ability to absorb life energy directly from a living being. These powerful vampires, called Vlads, still have fangs and can enjoy a blood meal, but they can also sustain themselves with simple skin-to-skin contact. The truly powerful, like I suspected the Magister was, didn't even need that and could simply sip the energy from a nearby source. I had no intention of being anyone's snack food. Luckily, another thing that had been instilled in me from a young age by Gran, was personal shields. Not only did they help ground me when doing what little magic I could, they also protected me from energy sucking ghosts and Vlads.

45

"So, do tell me Miss Harry Russo, how does a lovely, young lady such as yourself come to be called *Harry?*" Salvador looked at me with reappraising eyes. "Surely it must be short for something? Harriet perhaps? Although in truth, I don't think that is much better. No, something else then. Hermoine?"

"It's Angharad, but please, everyone calls me Harry. I –"

"Angharad! How delightful. You never hear the old names anymore." He turned to look at Nash. "Why Cian, we have another Celt in our midst." He laughed heartily like it was some great joke then raised his glass. "*Slainte! Salud!*" He emptied his glass and then returned it to the low table in front of him with a bang. "So what can I do for you my lovely Miss Russo?"

I quickly stole a glance at Nash. He glared back at me. There would be hell to pay with him when this was all over. "I...I'm here on behalf of Bryce Chow, or that is to say his sister, Bianca."

Nash grumbled something and I shifted uncomfortably, trying to avoid making eye contact.

"Ah yes, the recently departed Mr. Chow." Salvador shook his head in exaggerated sadness. "Taken so young and before he paid off his sister's debt." His eyes took on a calculating look. "And you are here to perhaps renegotiate?"

"No, well, I mean yes." I pulled the memory stick from my pocket and held it up. "Do you know what is on this?"

Salvador leaned forward, his interest piqued. "Do you?"

"Yes." I risked a quick look at Nash. He was pissed. "I believe that Bryce, uh, Mr. Chow, had already spoken to you in regards to a renegotiation of his

46

sister's debt before he was murdered. You agreed to cancel the debt in exchange for the video on this memory stick."

"I see." Salvador sat back, his hands steepled together, deep in thought. "And you wish to uphold that deal?"

"Yes, but with two additional stipulations." I took a deep breath to try and calm myself. "First, you will ban Bianca for life from all of your gambling establishments to ensure that a new debt is not incurred and you will promise to take no additional reprisals against her or any of Bryce's extended family; and second, you will pay for a funeral for Bryce. And not just some bargain service. It should be handled by...." I stopped and thought for a moment. "I've delivered flowers at one time or another to every funeral home in the city. "Brinkmans. Their silver service should do nicely I think."

Salvador made a show of thinking over the terms. "These demands are acceptable, even admirable, but you want nothing for yourself?"

"No. I'm not here for me. Besides, what was recorded on this video is totally abhorrent and should be stopped. You're the Magister. It should be your concern."

"You have seen what is in the video?"

"Yes."

"And you understand what you saw?"

"Yes, unfortunately." I couldn't stop the shiver that travelled down my spine.

"Very well. Give us the video. Once it has been verified, the debt shall be considered paid."

"I would prefer to have the promissory note signed off now."

"You doubt the word of the Magister?"

I had almost forgotten about Tomas, he had been sitting there so quietly. Not so now. He jumped up from his seat and took a menacing step towards me. From the corner of my eye I saw Nash tense as if ready to jump to my defense.

"Why should we deal with you when we can simply take what we want?" Tomas sneered at me.

The memory stick disappeared from my hand, leaving me gasping in surprise. Tomas held the stick up triumphantly. Either he was really fast, or had some sort of telekinetic gift.

"It seems you no longer have anything we need," he mocked.

I shrugged to convey how unconcerned I felt at his threat. "Perhaps, provided you know how to decrypt a 128-bit password. Or, you could cancel the debt and pay for Bryce's funeral and I could give you the key to the encryption. Your call."

Tomas frowned and then grabbed a nearby laptop. He inserted the key. A few moments later he looked at Salvador and shook his head. Salvador clapped his hands and laughed heartily. "Ah, Miss Russo, well played. Well played indeed."

Chapter Eight

I managed to get the hell out of there several minutes later. We settled on a handshake and a promise that I would courier the encryption token first thing the next morning. I figured it was better to just take Salvador's word rather than press the issue. He was after all the Magister and a vampire, and vampires could get pretty uppity about someone breaking their word. Besides, the atrocity that had been captured on the video had to be stopped before anyone else died. Even if Salvador hadn't agreed to my terms, I would have ended up giving it to him.

Tess rushed to my side the moment I exited the stairs. "Omigod! What took you so long? I was totally freaking out, especially when I saw Nash go up behind you."

I grabbed Tess's arm intent on making a quick getaway, until what she'd said registered. "Wait a minute. How do you know who Nash is?" I looked at her and her eyes darted away. There definitely was something she wasn't telling me about a certain surly cop, but at this point I really didn't care to hang around and find out what it was. "Come on. Let's get out of here."

Outside the club, the line had gotten considerably longer and the night felt a lot colder on my bare skin. We were hurrying along the sidewalk towards Tess's car, when a hulking shape stepped out of the shadows.

"You and I need to talk."

"Shit!" I stopped with my hand already reaching for my katana, until I realized it was Nash. "Damn it, Detective! Are you trying to give us a heart attack?"

Nash continued to stand and scowl, arms folded across his chest, blocking our path. "I mean it, you and I need to have a conversation," he practically growled the words at me. "And you," he pointed at Tess, "what were you thinking?"

Tess practically cowered at his words. What had happened to my feisty Chihuahua and who did this guy think he was yelling at my friend? "Look, it's been a long day and I'm tired and just want to go home. You can bawl me out tomorrow." I grabbed Tess's arm again and started to go around him.

"Bawl you out? I should..." He stopped and looked around then lowered his voice, "I should arrest you for withholding evidence."

Was he serious? This was getting out of hand. I held my hands up to him, fists clenched, wrists together, daring him to slap the cuffs on. "Fine. Arrest me. Maybe I'll get a nice, quiet jail cell to sleep in. You have nothing to charge me with and you know it."

Nash grabbed one of my hands and pulled me closer. "I'm not going to arrest you, but we *are* going to talk. You ride with me." He started to pull me the opposite direction from where I wanted to go.

"Listen you Neanderthal, I already have a ride." I wrenched my hand from his and gestured to Tess, expecting her to chime in and come to my defense. Instead, she shook her head and looked down at her boots.

"I'll deal with you later," Nash growled at Tess. "Go home."

Tess quickly turned and scurried off towards her car. "What the hell, Tess? Thanks a lot," I called after her. I couldn't believe she had just abandoned me.

Nash reached for my hand again and twined his fingers with mine. He seemed to have calmed down a little. "Come on. I'll take you home," he started walking back towards the club, dragging me along, "and then we'll talk."

We walked back past the entrance to the club in silence, Nash still holding my hand. I don't know whether it was because he forgot he was doing it or he was afraid I might bolt, but it felt kind of nice, so I didn't complain. We came to a side street and Nash stopped in front of a motorcycle. It had a split 2-up seat with a tiny little grab bar over the back fender.

"Oh no, you don't expect me to ride on the back of that?" I gestured to the bike.

"What's the matter....chicken?" Nash grinned. "You obviously have a death wish. This should be right up your alley." He straddled the bike and fired it up. "Get on."

Not seeing much of an alternative - my ride had deserted me and there was little chance of hailing a cab at this time of night - I kicked down the foot peg meant for the passenger and climbed on. To say it was awkward is an understatement. I mean are all biker chicks short or something? I felt like I was all knees and elbows as I tried to find a way to hang on for my life without actually touching Nash.

Finally, having lost what little patience he had left, or maybe he just took pity on me, Nash grabbed my arms and pulled me close, wrapping them around his mid-section. I tensed, but then he growled, "you'd better hang on" so I let myself relax against him. I barely had a moment to appreciate the heat coming off him or the flat, washboard abs I could feel beneath my hands, when the bike roared to life and took off down

51

the lane. I'm not ashamed to admit it, I squealed like a girl in surprise.

***

Ever heard the expression 'like a bat out of hell'? The person that coined the phrase must have ridden on the back of a motorcycle with Cian Nash. He drove as if speed limits were more like suggestions and the right of way was his. Always. I finally just buried my face against his shoulder and held on for dear life.

When we arrived at the firehall, I practically fell off the bike in my haste to get my feet on solid ground. My hair was a windswept mess and my cheeks were numb with the cold. The parking lot was empty except for my beat up old Chevy truck. No surprise that we beat Tess home with the way Nash, the maniac, drove. I shot a quick "thanks for the ride" over my shoulder and sprinted up the stairs to the second storey entrance.

My hopes that Nash might just drive off and leave me alone were dashed when instead of the sound of the door slamming behind me, I heard the clomping of motorcycle boots as they followed me inside. I scowled at Nash and he scowled right back, but seemed to be opting for the silent treatment. Fine by me.

Nash followed me further into the apartment and did the one thing everyone did when they saw it for the first time. He walked over to check out the fireman's pole that had a prominent place between the kitchen and the dining area. The pole ran up to the third level through a circular hole in the ceiling. Actually the pole ran through all three stories, from the third floor right down to my shop below, but we had sealed up the floor around it on the second level. The pole was more a conversation piece than anything, although I admit that both Tess and I used it on occasion as a quick way to get from the third floor hallway to the kitchen.

I pulled off my leather jacket, feeling slightly uncomfortable at how much bare skin was revealed, and unclasped the harness for my katana. Nash's eyes widened at the sight of the two foot blade.

"Do you know how to use that thing?"

The condescension in his voice set my teeth on edge, but I ignored it, turning my back on him to hang the precious blade on the wall. I grabbed a hooded sweatshirt from the hook by the door and pulled it on. Walking to the kitchen, I deftly unhooked and removed the leather contraption underneath the sweatshirt as I went. Only when it and the dog collar were piled on the kitchen counter and I felt much less restricted, did I reply.

"I can hold my own."

"Hold your own?" The condescension had been replaced once again with anger. "You are so over your head." He ran a hand through his hair in frustration. "Do you even know what you've done?"

"Done? I've brought a dangerous and horrific act to the attention of the proper authority and I've helped out someone who needed it."

"No, what you've done is brought *yourself* to the attention of the most dangerous man in the city. Do you realize the danger you put yourself in tonight? Not to mention breaking and entering a crime scene earlier today." Oh, so he had somehow figured out I had been there at Bryce's.

"I can take care of myself. I knew what I was doing." I came to stand in front of him. He had a good eight inches on me, but in my Doc Martens, I at least didn't have to strain my neck to look into his eyes.

"Look, I appreciate your concern, but I had everything under control."

As I turned away from him, his hand shot out to grab my arm. "You're not as smart as I thought you were, if you think you stand a chance against a vampire."

That was it. Enough was enough. Just who did this guy think he was? Drawing on my six plus years of martial arts training and double that in self-defence techniques, I grabbed his hand by the thumb and used his own momentum to twist it around. With just my grasp on his thumb, I had him helpless and kneeling on the floor, his arm twisted painfully behind his back in two seconds flat. It was the same move I had used on Neville. "I told you I can hold my own."

I released him almost immediately, turning my back on him, only to find myself swept off my feet and pinned to the floor, my breath knocked out of me.

"Never turn your back on your enemy."

Winded, I looked up into his eyes, surprised to find not anger but genuine concern. "Are you my enemy?" I asked a bit breathlessly.

The moment was broken by the sound of steps outside the door. I used the distraction of Tess's arrival home to escape. Pulling my arms to my sides and then pushing up on his chest, I scissored my legs up and knocked him to the floor beside me. I quickly straddled him and threw an open-handed palm to his face stopping just before I would have made contact and broken his nose. I jumped to my feet and backed away from him.

The three of us stood staring at each other until Tess dropped her eyes and looked away. Nash continued to stare at her angrily.

"What the hell is your problem?" I turned to glare at Nash. "She lives here. There's no need to growl..." I paused, my eyes going wide as the pieces fell into place. I looked from Tess and back to Nash. "That's it, isn't it? You *are* practically growling...growling like a big, angry..."

"Harry..." Tess pleaded.

"... dog. You're one of them," I went on ignoring Tess, knowing the dog comment wasn't going to do me any favours. I can't believe I didn't see it before. If there was ever an alpha male, it was Cian Nash.

"You told her?" Nash took a step towards Tess, who cowered even more.

I stepped between them and pushed at Nash with my hands on his chest. "Of course I know. We live together, grew up together. It's a little hard to hide the fact that you go all furry with the full moon."

Nash scowled at my furry comment. That's another thing werewolves don't like, being reminded that no matter how much control they may have over their shape change, all bets were off at the full moon.

"I had permission to tell her," Tess mumbled, not looking up.

That was news to me, but I'd go with it. "Yeah, she had permission so stand down. You. Big. Bully." I accentuated each word with a push against Nash's chest, none of which made him budge an inch. I'd never seen Tess so cowed. Of course I had never seen her with another werewolf except her uncle. His gym was mainly used by humans, not werewolves, and when it was used by the pack, it was closed to the public. On a whole, most werewolves didn't bother to work out. I guess getting furry and running around on all fours chasing rabbits once a month was enough to keep you fit.

I crossed my arms and glared at Nash, who in turn glared at Tess. Finally, I couldn't take it anymore and I threw up my hands in disgust. I stomped over to the computer and grabbed the copy of the video I had made.

"Here. I made you a copy. Take it. Maybe there's something on there you can use, but good luck explaining it to the norms you work with." I grabbed Nash's hand and pushed the memory stick into it. "Now, will you please just leave?"

Nash shoved the memory stick into his pocket. "Fine, I'm going. But this conversation isn't over."

"Yeah, whatever. Don't let the door hit you on the ass on the way out."

Chapter Nine

My body felt like it was on fire. His mouth moved along my abdomen, blazing a trail south. My back arched in anticipation. Kisses rained down on my skin, setting every molecule alight. I writhed, my hands skimming my body until they reached my breasts. Cupping each mound, I rubbed my nipples with my thumbs. Aching for more, my hand slid down between my legs to join his.

"What the hell?!"

I jolted awake and sat up in bed, flicking on the light to find an almost solid Bryce standing at the end of my bed.

"Whoa. I didn't even know I could do that." He held his hands up to look at them but they were quickly becoming more and more translucent. "How did I do that?"

"More like, what the hell did you think you were doing?" I grabbed a t-shirt from the end of the bed and pulled it on to cover the fact that I was sleeping buck naked.

Looking sheepish, Bryce shrugged. "I...well, you...."

"You don't just sneak into women's beds and start feeling them up, you pervert."

"But you looked like you were having such a good time." He wrapped his arms around himself and started to rub his shoulders while cooing, "Ooo, yeah. Ohhh baby..."

"Shut up. I was not doing that." I pulled the covers up over my legs. "What are you still doing here anyway? Didn't you see a light or something? I took care of your problem. You should be gone."

"I don't know. I was just here and you were sleeping..."

"So you decided to watch me? That's just creepy."

"Well, now that we know I can do more than watch..." He wiggled his eyebrows at me.

"No! That's just so wrong. Forget it, Bryce." I threw a pillow at him. It sailed right through his less than substantial body. "Why can't you just make yourself useful and try to remember who killed you?"

"I'm trying, but it's just not there. I can remember that I had accidentally left something at a job and I had gone back to get it, but then," he bumped his fist on his head in frustration, "I just don't know. I can't remember anything after that."

"Okay. It's all right." I looked at the clock. Four thirty a.m. Great. I'd only been asleep for an hour and a half. "I'm going back to sleep. We'll try and figure it out in the morning."

Bryce took a step towards the bed. "You know I could..." He held up his hands and wiggled his fingers, a cheeky smile on his face.

I leaned over and gestured for him to come closer then zapped him with 1200 volts from the Taser I grabbed from the bedside table. Unable to withstand the power overload, he instantly evaporated into thin air. "No means no, you pervert."

***

Hours later, I still couldn't get the dream out of my head. Sure it was sexy and a girl has needs, but I was having a hard time understanding why the co-star of my own personal mind-porn had to be Cian Nash. Okay, so the guy was hot, sexy hot; gorgeous green eyes, tousled hair, washboard abs and chiseled biceps hot. But he was also a jerk, a great big, A-one, alpha jerk.

As if I needed more proof of that, Tess arrived home from the gym for lunch with a pronouncement.

"Tonight? The Triad wants to see me tonight?" I asked incredulously. After years of being barred from werewolf affairs, suddenly the Triad, the pack's ruling council, wanted to see me. This couldn't be good. "It's Nash, isn't it? He ratted you out and now you're in trouble or something?"

"No, of course not." Tess looked uncomfortable. "Look, the Triad just thought it was time. They want to meet you." She turned away and started fussing with her gym bag. "I've got to head back to work. Don't worry, it'll be fun. You and Holly have been wanting to come to The Lodge and now you'll get your chance."

There was definitely more to it than what Tess was letting on. We were close, like sisters, except when it came to all things werewolf. It stemmed back to the year we turned sixteen. Gran had passed away and just when we needed each other the most, Tess disappeared from my life for six months. I knew it had to do with the fact that her first change had occurred, werewolves don't shift for the first time until after puberty kicks in, but it still hurt to suddenly be shut out. It was a big part of her life - it defined who she was - but she wasn't allowed to share it with me or Holly and it put a strain on all of us. Whatever it was that was bugging Tess, I let it slide. I'd find out soon enough when I met the Triad tonight. Besides, she was right, Holly and I had been dying to see The Lodge, the infamous werewolf bar.

With no deliveries needed for the shop and Holly and Tess both at work, I had spent my time staring at the computer watching the video over and over, hoping to find some clue to the identities of the men. There was also something different about the knife they used. It looked like some sort of ceremonial dagger and I wondered if it might provide a lead. The video was just too grainy to be much use though, because of the low lighting, and I didn't know how to fix it.

"The quality of the video is crap." Bryce materialized beside me, sitting on the desk.

"Thanks, Captain Obvious. Can I do anything to clean it up?"

"Well, you could try to punch up the highlights, maybe neutralize the colour balance, stabilize – "

"Forget I asked." I shook my head. I had no clue how to do what he was talking about.

"Here let me..." He reached for the mouse, only to have his hand pass through. "Oh yeah, forgot about that." He playfully pushed his spectral hand into the side of the computer until it disappeared up to his wrist then pulled it out again. "Hmmmm, maybe I could...." He grabbed both sides of the computer then appeared to bang his head on the case. Instead, his head disappeared followed quickly by his shoulders then arms, and then suddenly he was gone.

"Bryce!" I looked at the computer monitor. The normal desktop had been replaced by a black screen with a blinking cursor. "Bryce?"

HEY. THIS IS SO COOL.

The words appeared on the screen where the blinking cursor had been.

"Bryce?" I looked at the monitor in surprise. "Are you in my computer?"

YES. WHAT A PIECE OF CRAP. YOU'RE USING A 10 YEAR OLD OPERATING SYSTEM? SERIOUSLY?

"Whoa. I didn't know you could do that."

NEITHER DID I. DID I MENTION THIS IS SO COOL? HEY! I'M NO LONGER A SPIRIT IN THE MATERIAL WORLD. I'M A GHOST IN THE MACHINE!

Man, that was bad. "Police album references aside, do you think you can fix the video?"

YES. BUT WE'RE GOING TO NEED SOME UPGRADES FIRST.

"Upgrades?"

DON'T WORRY ABOUT IT. I'LL TAKE CARE OF EVERYTHING.

More famous last words.

Chapter Ten

I spent the remainder of the afternoon tending my rooftop garden. I may have a magical green thumb, thanks to inheriting some witchy powers from Gran, but the plants still needed some hands on care. This late in the season, most gardeners had already brought in their harvest and packed it in for the year. Not me though, with the help of my magic I would be gardening all year long.

When the sun began to set, I arrived back in my room to take a shower, just in time to hear the tail end of a phone message from our landlord.

"....so sorry. So very sorry. Goodbye."

I grabbed the phone hoping to catch him. "Hello? Mr. Rahmadesh?" He had already hung up. That was strange. I wondered what he could be calling about. It was the middle of the month and the rent wasn't due until the first. And, what did he have to be sorry about?

I called his cell but got that annoying 'We're sorry the cellular customer you have dialed is not available' message. Weird. Weirder still, when I tried his shop number - he owned the local dry cleaners - the message said the phone had been disconnected. I was sure there would be an explanation though. Mr. Rahmadesh had probably switched service providers or something. I'd listen to his entire message later after I jumped in the shower.

***

I was never getting out of the shower again. Being swathed by hot water flowing out of multi-jets and a rain head shower will do that to you. Definitely worth the splurge I had made in my ensuite bathroom.

Since our bedrooms were side by side, Tess and I had opted to both have smaller private ensuites with showers and share a large bathroom between our two rooms with a great, big, jetted soaker tub.

"You've got visitors," a voice said from outside of the shower stall.

"Gran! Where have you been?" I spluttered as I got a face full of water. I fumbled for the faucet and turned the water off. Grabbing a towel, I wrapped it around myself and stepped out of the shower. "It's been crazy around here thanks to that stupid date – "

"We don't have time for chit chat right now. You have company downstairs. Get dressed."

"Company? Who? What's going on?" I dried myself off quickly and hurried into my bedroom.

"I don't know, but if *he's* here, nothing good. Where's your sword?"

"Where it always is, hanging up downstairs. Who's he? Why do I need my sword? Should I call the police?"

"The police won't help you. Laws don't touch him. How he found you, I don't know."

"Found me? Who found me?" I quickly pulled on some jeans and a t-shirt. "What's going on?"

"Salvador Arroyo. The Magister. I don't know how he found out about you...."

"The Magister? Here? Why would he be here? *How* could he be? He's a vampire."

Just like in the movies, a vampire had to be invited across your threshold. That was the main reason we had closed off the access to the apartment from the shop using the fire pole. As a public business, a vamp could enter the shop with no restrictions. We wanted to make sure the apartment was a completely separate space. Vampires may be sticklers for the rules, but they were also great at finding loopholes. I palmed a knife that I sometimes carried. Not that it would do much good against a vampire, but a six-inch, double-edged, clip point blade was better than nothing and I didn't own a gun or silver bullets.

I had more questions for Gran, like how she knew the Magister and why he would even be looking for me, but she conveniently had vanished. I quickly texted an SOS to Tess to let her know I had company, then quietly made my way to the top of the stairs leading down to the second level. The stairs came out at the end of the hall behind the kitchen. There were no sightlines into the living area from the bottom of the stairway which meant that whoever was downstairs wouldn't be able to see me; then again, I wouldn't be able to see them either.

I crept as quietly as I could, but it was pretty much a given that I couldn't hide from a vampire's amped up hearing or sense of smell. When I reached the end of the wall dividing the hall and the kitchen, I started to peek around the corner only to be abruptly grabbed and thrown against the wall.

"Gaak!" I said. Hey, you try talking when a six foot goon with the strength of a vampire has his arm across your windpipe.

Tomas had pinned my knife hand as well as my throat. He grinned at me smugly. I could see Salvador lounging unconcerned across the room. My vision began to blur from the lack of oxygen as I let my knees give out a little, shifting more of my weight onto his arm. Surprised, he loosened his grip enough that I was able to take a rasping breath. I quickly brought my knee up to his groin as hard as I could. It was satisfying to know that whatever he was, he still felt it when he got one in the 'nads. Tomas let go of my arm and I slid down the wall. Unwilling to hope that a shot to the junk was enough to keep him down, I followed through with a quick punch to his throat. He fell to one knee and I sprang away trying to get across the room to my katana.

I only made it a couple steps before Tomas grabbed my ankle and sent me sprawling on my back. With the lightning speed of an angry vampire, I was once again pinned. This time Tomas knelt over me straddling my hips, his one hand on my collarbone, the other in my hair pulling my head back to expose my throat.

"I'm going to enjoy sucking you dry." He bared his teeth, his fangs prominently displayed. What the hell was he? I could feel his body heat and the thumping of his heart in his chest, but he had fangs and the strength and speed of a vamp.

"I wouldn't recommend that," I rasped, my voice steadier than I would have expected, given the circumstances. "Not unless you want to see who bleeds out first." To emphasize my point, I pushed the tip of my knife up against his groin. Whatever Tomas was, I was hoping he would bleed. "It would be a shame to slice up your nice pants; although, black leather? Really? Isn't that a little much for this time of day?"

Tomas hissed and I tensed waiting for him to tear out my throat. Instead of the intense pain I expected, there was the sound of three slow claps.

"Children, children," Salvador admonished. "Enough playing games."

With another hiss, Tomas released his grip on my head, just as I started to push him off me. I sprang to my feet and completed my dash across the room, grabbing my katana and unsheathing it in one motion.

"What the hell are you doing in my house?" I positioned myself with my back to the wall, keeping both vampires in sight at the end of my blade. "How did you even get in here? You haven't been invited."

"You mean *my* house." Salvador waved his hand to encompass the room.

"Your house?" I stammered, but I already knew what he meant, the half-heard phone message from my landlord suddenly making frightening sense. "What did you do to Mr. Rahmadesh?"

"Do?" Salvador smiled, pressing his hands together as if in prayer. "Why I did nothing to your dear Mr. Rahmedash, but offer him a proposal he felt he couldn't refuse."

"Why? Why would you want to buy this building?"

"Come now. Must you stand there? Sit, sit. We mean you no harm." Salvador gestured to the chair beside him.

I looked at Tomas who still stood glaring at me. "I think your friend here would beg to differ."

"Nonsense. Tomas will not harm you." When he spoke, I could feel the power behind his words. Tomas's stance stiffened and he looked away from me.

I lowered my sword but didn't re-sheathe it. "What do you want from me? I sent you the encryption key this morning."

"Yes, yes," he gestured impatiently. "That deal has been struck and it will be honoured. I come to you now with a different proposition."

I shifted uneasily. I was pretty sure I wasn't going to like the sound of whatever it was he was going to propose. "What *kind* of proposition?"

Salvador laughed. "Oh my dear Miss Russo, so suspicious. Relax. I promise you it is nothing you will find too," he paused as if trying to find the right words, "...unsavoury. A deal that will be mutually beneficial."

"I'm listening."

"One night," he held up a finger dramatically, "one night of your time." He raised his hand to stall my protests. "For dinner. You spend the evening with me, dine with me at my club, and in return, I will give you the deed to this building."

"Just like that? You'd hand over a half million dollar building for a dinner date?" I eyed him suspiciously. There had to be a catch, there was always a catch when it came to making deals with vampires. Like maybe I would *be* dinner.

"I assure you there is no catch." Salvador replied. It was as if he read my mind, which did little to set me at ease. For all I knew he *could* read my mind. If that was the case, then if Salvador thought I was going to have sex with him, he could take the deed to the building and shove it....Hmm, no response there. So maybe Salvador couldn't read my mind.

"Don't get me wrong, I want my building, but I don't see what you get out of the deal." Figuring I was safe enough and, since I felt stupid standing there holding my katana, I sheathed it, but didn't hang it back up.

"Why your charming conversation of course." Salvador managed to say it with a completely straight face so I was almost inclined to believe he meant it, especially when I looked over at Tomas, who appeared to be having an aneurysm or something. The look on Tomas's face alone might have been worth the date.

"We have so much to talk about, you and I," Salvador continued on, seemingly oblivious to his Lieutenant's distaste at the thought. "I find you most intriguing. Why have we not met before?" He paused to look at me appraisingly. "And then of course, there's that nasty business on the video you provided to me."

"You've watched the video? Do you know who the men are?" I was eager to learn what I could, in case it helped lead us to Bryce's killers.

"Yes, yes, all in due time. Shall we say nine o'clock, tomorrow evening?" Salvador rose from his seat. He reached into the breast pocket of his three piece suit and pulled out an official looking piece of paper. "And as a show of good faith, I have already taken the liberty of signing the building over to you. Let us shake hands and call it a deal, shall we?"

I looked at the deed and then Salvador's outstretched hand. There had to be a catch. Just like the saying, if it was too good to be true...there was probably a vampire involved.

"Just dinner and conversation, nothing else. And, I get to come home, safe, afterwards?" I hesitated.

"Yes, you will be perfectly safe. It is simply dinner and conversation, and the building is yours, free and clear." If there was more, he didn't get a chance to say it before someone began to bang on the door.

"Miss Russo! Harry! Open up. It's Detective Nash."

"Well my dear?" Salvador arched an eyebrow at me. "Do we have a deal?"

"I..." I looked to the door then back to Salvador, "...yes." I reached out and he grasped my hand firmly.

Unlike our handshake from the other night, this time I felt a tingling sensation followed by a sense of well-being. Salvador bowed over my hand, turning it palm up to press his lips against the pulse throbbing in my wrist. Deep in the recesses of my mind, I knew that I had just made some sort of mistake, but it was hard to be concerned with such a warm and inviting feeling running through me.

"Harry! Are you there? We need to talk." Nash's voice broke through my reverie. I looked up, but Salvador and Tomas were already making their way to the door leaving me standing with the deed in one hand and my katana lying in its sheath on the floor beside me.

"Until tomorrow, my dear Miss Russo." Salvador smiled at me, looking like a Cheshire cat. Tomas opened the door, surprising Nash with his hand raised in mid-knock. "Detective Nash." Salvador nodded to Nash then proceeded out the door, followed by Tomas.

"Harry! Are you okay?" Nash rushed over, grabbing me by my elbows. He looked me up and down as if assessing me for injury, frowning at the red marks around my throat. "What the hell did he want? Did he hurt you?"

"What? No." I still felt a little dazed from my skin to skin contact with Salvador. "I...I shook his hand." I held up my hand to look at it. It looked absolutely normal. I swallowed in relief only to have the pain remind that someone *had* hurt me. I touched my throat. "It was that asshole, Tomas." The dazed feeling was quickly dissipating and I was getting my mad on instead. "What the hell is he anyway?"

"What is he? You mean you don't know?" Nash ran his hand through his hair. "No, of course you don't." There was something in his voice, more frustration than

69

anger, but it wasn't directed at me. He looked down at the paper in my hand. "Look, Tomas can wait. What else happened?"

"I made a deal with Salvador. He gave me the firehall." I stared incredulously at the deed. "He *gave* me the firehall. It's mine now. I own this building!"

"What? What do you mean?" Nash took the deed and looked it over. "What sort of deal?" He grabbed my arms again and gave me a shake. "What did you promise him?"

"Hey! Ouch!" I pushed him away. "Nothing, nothing! I just have to have dinner with him tomorrow. That's all."

"And you let him touch you? You shook his hand?"

"I..." Feeling uncertain, I looked at my hand again. "Yes, I shook his hand and he," I swallowed uncomfortably, "he kissed my wrist." I put my hand down quickly. "Look, it's no big deal. So he might have taken a little sip. I'm fine."

"No big deal?" He ran both hands through his hair. No wonder it always looked so tousled. "Don't you know what he can do with that one small taste?" At my puzzled look, he stormed on. "He will use that little taste to learn all he can about you. It's what he does, he's a Reader."

A Reader! No wonder Nash freaked out. Readers were rare. I had only ever read about them. With a drop of blood, or in this case a sip of my life essence, Salvador would know what magical gifts I had and how powerful they were or had the potential to be. He would know everything about me that I tried to keep secret, including some things I was trying to not admit even to myself. No wonder he was the Magister.

Readers made great leaders because they were able to recognize the talents of others and utilize everyone to their fullest potential.

I tried to downplay the issue. "So he knows that I'm a witch. That's no secret."

"And your *other* talents?" Nash frowned at me. "What about those?"

"I really don't know what you are talking about." At least I hoped I didn't, otherwise it meant someone, *Tess*, had blabbed about my little ghost problem.

Nash laughed. "Your poker face sucks. I know about the ghosts. I know that's how you found Bryce Chow's body and it's probably why you were in his apartment yesterday afternoon. You don't think that after your little stunt last night I wouldn't try and find out everything I could about you?"

"What I can or can't do is none of your business."

"It is when it becomes part of my murder investigation, and when it gets you in over your head and your safety becomes my concern."

"My safety is none of your concern. You're not my keeper. And, as far as your murder investigation goes, I've told you everything I know."

"What about everything Bryce knows?"

I shrugged. I didn't want to discuss Bryce with him. "He doesn't remember anything about his murder or about the video for that matter."

Nash looked around the room as if searching for something. "He's not here now is he?"

"Bryce? No."

"And your Grandmother?"

"Who told you about Gran?" As far as I knew, nobody knew about Gran except for Holly and Tess. The fact that your dead grandmother still haunted you seven years after her death wasn't exactly something you wanted to get around. It hurt to think that Tess had shared my secret.

Tess chose that moment to arrive home. She was winded like she had run the whole way from work.

"Harry! You're okay! That's a relief." She dropped her gym bag inside the doorway and then ran to give me a hug. "I was so worried when I got your text and I couldn't get away from the class I was teaching. That's why I called Nash."

I stiffened in her arms. "Yeah, you seem to have no problem blabbing everything about me to him."

"What?! I...Harry!" Ignoring Tess completely, I brushed past Nash and hurried upstairs to my room.

Chapter Eleven

"I can't believe I let you talk me into coming here tonight." I frowned at Holly. At her insistence I was keeping my meeting with the Triad even though I was in no mood for werewolf politics. We stood outside The Lodge, the pack's meeting place, a.k.a. party headquarters. Even growing up in an isolated community outside of the city, we had heard about The Lodge and the infamous parties that occurred there. Werewolves were notorious party animals, pun intended.

Tess stood quietly on the other side of Holly. We hadn't spoken since my little outburst and I was really in no mood to party even if I was dressed for it in a cute little Sherri Hill dress. Looking at The Lodge, I began to think the whole night would be a bust. It certainly didn't look anything like I expected pack party central to look like. It was a dive bar and we were seriously over-dressed.

Located out near the airport in an industrial park, The Lodge appeared to be housed in an old country roadhouse, complete with wooden shingle siding and a decaying wood-spoke wagon wheel hanging forlornly on the wall. It was wedged between two other apparently vacant buildings.

"Are you sure we're at the right place?" I looked at Holly who shrugged. I wasn't expecting a big neon sign proclaiming "PARTY HERE" or anything, but I hadn't been expecting a derelict building either. There weren't even any vehicles parked nearby and despite the empty street, Holly had made us park around the corner. For all intents and purposes, it looked like an abandoned building.

Tess pushed forward, striding towards the entrance. "Not everything is what is seems you know," she muttered.

With a shrug, Holly followed her. I didn't really want to be left standing alone in that neighbourhood, so I hustled in on Holly's heels.

The inside pretty much matched the outside in terms of décor, the tacky western saloon theme unfortunately continued, although it appeared to be a great deal cleaner and the lighting wasn't as dim as I expected. Despite its dated theme, you could tell that someone put an effort into maintaining the place, the wooden bar gleaming with polish. Maybe Tess was right, there was more to this place than what it seemed.

There were several booths hugging the perimeter of the room but the main seating was either at the bar itself or at one of the checkered-cloth tables, scattered in no discernable pattern across the space. The room was about half full and the low buzz of conversation came to a halt when Holly and I walked in the door.

I scanned the room. The faces didn't look threatening, but they didn't look all that friendly either. One in particular stared back at me, eyebrows raised in surprise. If I didn't know better, I'd think Nash was stalking me; although I guess technically, he had arrived first this time. He grumbled something and an attractive woman behind the bar swatted him on the arm. Someone called out, "Hey look, fresh meat," and his buddies guffawed along with him.

Holly, always happy to be the centre of attention, and how could she not be when wearing a leopard print halter top and a very short leather mini skirt, beamed and pranced up to the bar, "That's right boys, look out." She winked at a grizzled old man in a worn jean jacket sitting near the bar.

Tess rolled her eyes at me and I laughed, forgetting for a moment I was still supposed to be mad at her. She nodded to the woman drying glasses behind the bar. The tall brunette nodded back and said, "You're late." This seemed to be the cue to the rest of the room that we were accepted, because the tension eased and the buzz of conversation started up again.

"I'm sorry," Holly said, climbing onto a bar stool, "totally my fault. I couldn't decide what to wear." She held out her hand, "I'm Holly."

The striking woman behind the bar smiled and shook Holly's hand. "Eileen, Eileen Nash."

Surprised, I looked over to the where Nash sat at the opposite end of the bar. He was married? I wasn't sure why that bit of information should bother me, but it did.

Just then, another slightly older, attractive brunette came out through the swinging saloon doors behind the bar, carrying a steaming bowl in each hand. A delicious scent followed her as she weaved her way through the tables and set the bowls down in front of an older couple, reminding me that I hadn't really eaten much that evening. She wiped her hands on her apron and said, "Eat up. More where that came from," and then headed back towards the bar.

Eileen flagged her down and gestured to Holly. "Holly, this is my sister Christina. Christina, this is Holly and," she paused, looking at me.

"Harry. Harry Russo," I sputtered.

"Harry," Eileen smiled like I had said something amusing, "and of course, you remember Tess."

"Tess! About time you came to visit. It's been ages." Christina pulled Tess into a quick hug. Tess smiled sheepishly at her and shrugged. Smiling, Christina turned her attention to Holly and me. The resemblance to her younger sister, despite the age difference, was uncanny. "Holly," she nodded at Holly then turned to look at me appraisingly, "and Harry, a pleasure to finally meet you. My brother can't stop talking about you."

"Your brother?" I stole another look towards the end of the bar where Nash sat scowling into his beer. "I'm sure whatever he had to say was less than flattering." The sisters laughed and my stomach chose that moment to growl loudly.

"Gracious!" Christina put a hand to her cheek in mock surprise. "You sound as hungry as a wolf." She laughed at her own joke, then squeezed my hand. "Let's get you some stew. It's the house specialty. Don't want you drinking on an empty stomach." She turned and then disappeared through the tacky saloon doors.

"Speaking of drinking," Eileen pulled out a cloth and polished the already spotless bar in front of us, "what can I get you?"

We all settled on beers which Eileen expertly poured from the tap and placed in front of us. As was usual any time we went out with Holly, it wasn't long before she had gathered a little following of men around us. She was in her element, laughing and flirting, setting everyone at ease with her light banter.

When a cute blonde extended his hand and introduced himself to me as Joe, I couldn't help but notice the dark scowl on Nash's face. He had been watching us, looking stormier by the minute. I was sure he thought I shouldn't be there at all, seeing as how he seemed to believe that I was incapable of looking after myself. I began to take perverse pleasure in flirting with Joe, my hand resting on his arm after he made a particular witty remark, just to see Nash's face get darker.

During a lull in conversation, I looked around the bar. Something about the place was odd. Despite the fact that I'd noticed several more groups of people arrive since we sat down, the room never seemed to get any more crowded.

I said as much to Joe who laughed and replied, "Since it's your first time here, I guess you've never heard of the Ice House?"

"The what?"

"The Ice House. That's where the real fun happens. The bar here is just the front, where the oldsters hang out and where you get some of Christina's famous stew. But the real party is just getting started out back." He gestured to the back of the room to a door I hadn't noticed before. Werewolves were going through it in packs of two or three under the watchful eye of one of the biggest men I had ever seen. He was built like a tank, and now that I was paying attention, obviously acting as some sort of bouncer.

Joe leaned in close and ran his hand up my bare arm. "Do you like to dance?" he asked, his mouth close to my ear.

Before I could reply, there was a loud crash as Nash pushed himself away from the bar. His fallen stool had narrowly missed tripping Christina, who was just walking past with three bowls of hot stew balanced precariously.

Nash growled something then grabbed one of the bowls from Christina. He strode across the bar and the crowd around us parted. He clunked the bowl down in front of me and gruffly said, "Eat." Christina paused for a moment with a look of surprise on her face then set the other two bowls down in front of Tess and Holly.

"Mmmmm, smells delicious," Holly exclaimed.

Tess frowned, looking from the bowl in front of me to Nash and back again. She started to say something, but the look on Nash's face made her bite her lip and quickly look away.

"Oh for Pete's sake!" I had no clue what was going on, but the stew smelled delicious and I was starving. I picked up my spoon and dug in. Nash stomped away and the crowd, which a moment ago had seemed to be collectively holding their breath, resumed its activity.

***

The arrival of our food provided the cue to disperse Holly's admirers. Even Joe had melted away with the crowd.

"Oooo, did you see that hot guy with the beard?" Holly was talking a mile-a-minute and had barely touched her stew. "I can't wait to check out *his* moves." She gave me a little nudge and a wink. "And what about that Joe? He's a hottie. I bet he can shake it on the dance floor."

On the other side of Holly, Tess muttered something that sounded like 'ten-foot pole'.

"What?" Holly turned on her stool to look at Tess.

"Nothing." Tess slid down from her seat. "I'm going to run to the Ladies' while you finish up."

Something was definitely up with Tess. If I wasn't already angry with her, I probably would have been worried and tried to find out what was wrong, but I was angry, so I didn't.

Holly on the other hand, shot me an exasperated look and hopped off her stool to follow Tess. "Tess, wait up. I'll come with you." She shot another glare my way and then hurried off after a quickly retreating Tess.

"Good friends. They are a treasure."

The unfamiliar voice startled me and I turned to find a new face behind the bar, new, but somehow familiar. I looked around but neither Christina nor Eileen were anywhere to be seen. In fact, the area around us was suddenly deserted.

"I...yes, they are. I'm sorry, do I know you?"

The older woman laughed, her green eyes crinkling up at the corners. "We've met, but you were very young. I don't think you would remember." She extended her hand. "I'm Eleanor Nash. I knew your grandmother."

Another Nash! Now that she said it, I could see the family resemblance. Both Eileen and Christina had their mother's elegant beauty. And those green eyes - I could see where her son had gotten his.

"You knew Gran?"

"Yes, we were friends for many years." A look of sadness passed over her features. "I was very sorry to hear of her death," she raised an eyebrow and looked at me, "if not her passing."

I frowned, thinking of Tess and the secrets she had betrayed.

"Now, don't be too hard on young Tess." Her thoughts following mine, Eleanor reached out and squeezed my hand. "There isn't much a young wolf can keep from her elders." I felt a wave of power flow from her hand and the spidey-sense that allowed me to know such things started clanging loudly. Eleanor Nash was an extremely powerful werewolf. If she wasn't the pack's alpha, she was probably the next thing to it.

Anger made me reckless, despite the show of power I just witnessed, and I replied, "So you made Tess spy on me?"

"Spy? Nonsense. I prefer to think of it as helping me keep a promise to your grandmother." She patted my hand again and I pulled it away warily. "Your grandmother and I grew up together much like you and Tess."

I snorted. Gran was over ninety when she died, that would make Eleanor much older than she appeared. Frowning, I looked at her more closely. Sure her hair was streaked with grey and she had the wrinkles time brought with middle age, but ninety?

Eleanor laughed, her smile making her appear even younger. "It's not polite to ask a lady her age, but surely you know we wolves are long-lived?"

Determined not to be distracted from my anger, I huffed, "That doesn't give you the right to meddle in other people's lives. Why did Tess come to live with Gran and me? Was it so she could be your spy one day?" The more I thought about it, the more incensed I became.

"I've already told you, Tess is not my spy." Eleanor's eyes became steely, but I was no wolf; I didn't have to bow in subordination to her alpha. "Like you, Tess was an orphan; she needed a loving home. Yes, she could have been raised within the pack, but your grandmother was my friend and she was already raising another young girl. When she offered to take Tess out of friendship, I accepted." She fixed me with a knowing stare. "Would you rather I had not?"

"What?! No, of course not. Tess is my friend, more than my friend. She's my sister." I felt worse by the minute, thinking about how I had treated Tess earlier. I turned my anger outward to the real source of the recent trouble between Tess and me and glared at Eleanor. Damn wolf politics. Tess was no match for Eleanor's alpha wolf status. She would have had no choice but to answer any questions Eleanor asked about me. "Why do you even care about me anyway? You, the Magister...suddenly I'm Miss Popularity."

Eleanor frowned. "I didn't disagree with your grandmother about many things, but some decisions she made..." She paused and shook her head. "Ah well, a promise must be kept." She patted my hand again in a motherly fashion. "I think deep down you know. Perhaps you aren't yet ready to admit it even to yourself."

Now it was my turn to frown. Eleanor's comments had come a little too close to the mark, but I pushed those thoughts aside, focusing on my anger instead. My life was my business and nobody else's. And, I wasn't going to stand by while Tess was forced to use our friendship to glean information for the pack.

"No one uses my friends against me." I said vehemently. "If you think you need to know something about me, do me the courtesy of asking me."

Eleanor arched an eyebrow. "You remind me of your grandmother. She was fiercely loyal to her friends and always stood up for herself too. I can see why my son is so interested in you."

Say what? Nash, interested in me? The only interest he had was in making my life difficult. I looked at Eleanor in surprise, speechless.

"But here are your friends." Eleanor gestured to where Holly and Tess stood unsure whether or not to approach. "You should go have fun." Eleanor shooed me off.

"I can't. I'm supposed to meet with the Triad."

"You just did, dear." Eleanor chuckled. "Well, at least one of them."

"You're...but..." I looked at Eleanor in surprise.

"Now that wasn't so bad, was it? Surely not as frightening as meeting the Magister."

I looked at Eleanor, remembering the wave of power I felt from her earlier, and replied, "I think you can be just as scary as the Magister when you want to."

"Yes, of course dear. It's nice to know your grandmother didn't raise a fool."

Chapter Twelve

The party at the Ice House was in full force when we arrived. We didn't have to go far to get there, just pass inspection by the bouncer appropriately named Tank, and walk through the door at the back of the bar. The door led to a small storage room that served as the entrance to the Ice House; an old, formerly refrigerated warehouse behind the building that housed The Lodge.

The space itself was about the size of a hockey rink and could easily hold a couple hundred people. It was set up with a large dance floor in the middle and a bar running down either side. At the far end of the dance floor there was a DJ booth and a few tables for those wanting to sit. At the opposite end, near where we entered, a pool hall of sorts had been set up with four big green-felted tables, a couple of dart boards and overhead lighting.

Music blasted through the entire space, the throbbing beat so loud you could feel it pulse. No thrasher rock here; instead, it sounded like all the top 40 dance tunes were on the playlist.

The crowd was almost completely made up of werewolves of indiscriminate age. Unlike vampires, werewolves tended to be insular, socializing amongst themselves, although I could sense a few fellow witches in the crowd. The one thing I was sure I wouldn't find was a vampire. There were always some wolves wanting to push the envelope and party at Dante's or one of the other vampire clubs downtown, but you would never find a vampire wanting to 'slum it' at a werewolf club, not that they would be allowed to in any case.

The energy in the place was palpable and I shivered and took a deep breath, feeling it radiate over me in waves. I slammed my personal shields down against the onslaught, but even protected as I was, I could feel the energy taking hold, amping me up. It was seductive.

"Let's party!" I shouted over the music.

"Woo eee!" Holly replied, as she grabbed my arm and pulled me through the crowd towards the bar. "Let's fuel up. Then we dance our asses off!" She ordered three shots of tequila. We raised our shot glasses and I caught Tess's eye.

"To great friends who love you even when you act like a complete bitch."

Tess clinked her glass with mine and replied, "I'll drink to that as long as you're the bitch in the scenario."

"Yay! To friends!" shouted Holly. "Kiss and make up you two."

We tossed back our drinks and Tess and I threw our arms around each other, relieved that the rift between us was mended.

"I'm sorry I gave you such a hard time. I know you didn't have a choice," I said.

"I'm sorry too, Harry. I only told them what I absolutely had to."

"Well, hopefully it won't be an issue anymore. If the Triad needs to know something about me they can just ask me their damn selves."

"Harry! You didn't say that to Eleanor did you?"

I shrugged. "Sort of."

"Enough you two! Let's go dance!" Holly grabbed our hands and pulled us to the dance floor. The crowd parted around us, making room. At first, I just let go and the three of us danced together, like female friends can do, not caring about anything else, just having a good time. After a while, I looked up and noticed that both Holly and Tess had managed to gather some male admirers. That's when I noticed that I was dancing alone. There was a gap in the crowd all around me. At first I thought it was some sort of anomaly of crowd dynamics but when I moved, the gap followed me. It was like the crowd was the greasy dishwater and I was a drop of detergent. Everyone on the dance floor seemed to be making an effort to stay at least two feet away from me, especially those with a Y chromosome.

To test my theory, I scanned the crowd until I saw a familiar face. It was Joe. He was dancing on the far side of the crowd. I made my way over to him, which wasn't difficult since the crowd parted before me like the Red Sea did for Moses, and caught his eye.

"Hey handsome, ready for that dance?"

"What?" Joe looked around nervously. "Uh, no. Sorry," he continued, looking over his shoulder again. "I was just going." He pushed his way through the crowd, leaving me standing there dumbfounded.

"Harry! Hey, Harry!" Holly plowed through the crowd towards me. "Where are you going?"

"Looks like nowhere." I turned my head and sniffed my shoulder. "Is there something wrong with me? Do I smell or something?"

"What are you talking about?"

"Does my breath smell?" I lifted my palm in front of my mouth and exhaled on it.

Holly grabbed my arm. "What on earth has gotten into you? Are you drunk?"

I pulled my arm from her grasp. "No, of course not. But I think I'm a leper or something." I looked down at my dress with its cute ruffled skirt. "Is Gran right? Is it my clothes? Do I really look like a hippy school marm?"

"Are you kidding? You look gorgeous in that dress." Holly began pulling me towards a table. "Here, sit down." She looked at me sternly. "Stay there. I'm going to get you some water. I think you must be dehydrated or something."

Holly arrived back, Tess in tow, a few minutes later. Even if she hadn't been carrying two shooters of tequila in each hand, I would have known from her expression that something was wrong.

"Here, drink this," she said, handing me a glass.

"What happened to the water?"

"Trust me, you're going to want this."

I shrugged and gulped the tequila back, grimacing as it burned its way down my throat. I sucked in a breath through my teeth and said, "Alright, whatever it is, lay it on me." I looked from Tess to Holly and then back again. They both looked like they were about to tell me that my dog died. I'd have been worried, but I don't own a dog. "Come on. Spill it. Don't keep me in suspense."

***

I knew that Tess had finished speaking because her lips had stopped moving, but frankly, I had stopped listening. Besides, it was hard to hear anything over the dull roar of the anger building inside my head.

"He did what?!" I stood up, pushing my chair over. "That bastard." I grabbed another shot of tequila and tossed it back, slamming the empty glass on the table. "Wait until I find him. I'll kill him." I pushed past Tess, who did her best to block my path.

"Harry, wait!" Holly made a lunge for my arm, but she was too slow. I was already storming across the dance floor, the crowd parting before me, which I now knew was thanks to Nash and his meddling. I didn't really have a plan or have a clue where I might find Nash. I just needed to move. By the time I had stomped my way across the dance floor, something that's not particularly easy in three inch pumps, some of my anger had worn off and the tequila had kicked in. It made for a dangerous combination, especially with the waves of energy already pounding at me. I relaxed my shields a little, letting a tendril of the pulsing wave slip past. It was like a drug, wrapping around me, heightening my senses, making me feel more alive. I stopped where I was and closed my eyes, relishing the feeling.

"Hey pretty lady. Why is a sweet thing like you all alone?"

I opened my eyes in surprise. The speaker was around my age, although with werewolves it's hard to tell, and as is typical with many of the non-human races, he was good looking bordering on smoking hot. Obviously he hadn't gotten the less than subtle message Nash had left earlier regarding me being off limits. Maybe he wasn't there when Nash brought me the stew, which in werewolf terms meant I was untouchable. It had some Neanderthal-like reasoning behind it which I had sort of tuned out when Tess was explaining things. It went something like since Nash fed me, I was his and no other wolves could touch me, unless they wanted to fight him for me first, or some such nonsense. Maybe this guy had a death wish. Whatever the case, I wasn't in the mood to pass up the opportunity.

"I'm not alone now." I ran my hand down his bare, muscular arm. "Dance with me." It was more a command than a question. I grabbed his hand and pulled him further onto the dance floor.

Between the lights and the music and the pulsing flow of energy, I felt a rush. My new friend pulled me close and whisper-shouted in my ear, "I'm Greg."

I smiled in answer and just kept dancing, the beat of the music hypnotic. I let it wash over me, flow into me, feeling like I was flying higher with each beat. The music changed to something sexy and seductive. Greg put his hands on my hips and we did a bump and grind, our bodies touching. I felt on fire. Feeling reckless, I reached up and ran my hand through his hair, pulling his mouth to mine. He responded to my kiss, his mouth exploring mine. He slid his hands down to cup my ass, pressing my body up against his.

"Are you nuts man?" The voice startled us. A hand reached out and grabbed Greg's arm, pulling us apart. A wolf I didn't recognize scowled at me then pulled Greg further away.

"What the fuck, Ethan?" Greg shrugged his friend off. Ethan grabbed his arm again and leaned in to whisper something in Greg's ear.

Greg stiffened and looked at me, putting his hands up as if to ward me off. "I'm sorry. I didn't know." He shook his head then backed further away.

"Wait. Stop." I reached out to him but he shied away. "I don't belong to anyone. You can dance with me if you want."

"Harry!" Tess came running up to me, Holly following close behind. "What's going on? Are you okay?"

"I'm fine! I'm just fine!" I brushed her off. "No, that's a lie. I'm not fine, I'm pissed off at Nash. Well, screw him. Can't you feel it? This place is electric. I feel like I could fly!" I threw my arms wide, soaking in the energy all around me. I felt giddy with it.

"Harry!" Holly grabbed my arms. "Stop that! You're going to overdo it."

"Oh, Holly, don't be such a spoilsport. I feel wonderful. Or I would except for that, that jack-off....no, ass-off.... I mean that jerk off, asshole Nash ruining my entire night!" I swayed, my knees buckling a little. "Whoa." I threw my hand out to steady myself against Tess. Okay, so maybe I was a little out of control.

"Harry, it's too much. You're drunk. High even." Holly looked at me with concern.

"Nah, I'm fine. I'm good." I closed my eyes, feeling the music pounding within me again. "I just want to dance only no one will dance with me, thanks to Nash." I pushed away from Tess and staggered to the edge of the dance floor.

Climbing onto a table, I scanned the crowd then cupped my hands to my mouth and shouted, "Nash! Cian Nash!" I looked out over the crowd. "Nash, you coward! Come out and face me like a man."

"Harry, have you gone crazy?" Holly tried to grab for me. "Get down before you fall and break your neck."

"Nonsense. I have perfect balance." I wobbled on the table. "See?"

"Harry, come on. You're going to hurt yourself." Tess came to stand beside Holly.

The crowd around us had stopped dancing and everyone milled around looking at us. Suddenly there was a movement at the back of the crowd and it parted, letting a very pissed off looking Nash pass.

"Oh, there you are. The big, bad wolf. Ha!" I shook my fist at him causing the table to wobble some more. "Whoa!" My foot slipped, but I quickly regained my balance.

"Harry, what the hell are you doing?" Nash strode up and stopped in front of me, hands on his hips. "Get down from there before you fall."

"You aren't the boss of me, you, you...Mister."

"Are you drunk?" Nash looked at Holly and Tess. "Is this how you take care of her?" Tess cowered away from him.

"Hey! Leave my friends alone, you big bully." I leaned over to try and push him away. The table wobbled again and I lost my footing, sending me flying off, straight into Nash's arms.

He quickly set me down on my feet. "Are you okay?" He held me out at arm's length so he could look at me.

"I'm fine." I closed my eyes for a moment to try and stop the room from spinning. "Okay, maybe I'm a little not so fine." I ran my fingers through my hair. "My head, it's just...." I made a blowing up hand gesture like my head was exploding outward. "Buhwow!" I laughed, my arms stretched over my head. "Can't you feel it?" I started to slow motion dance to the music.

"Are you high? Did you take something?" Nash grabbed me by my elbow pulling me through the crowd.

"Hey! Hold on." I tried to pry his fingers from my arm. "Let go of me!" He dragged me across the room and out a side door to a quiet hallway. Tess and Holly skidded through the door behind us.

"Are you on drugs?" He grabbed my face and looked at my eyes.

I slapped his hands away. "Stop that. I'm not on anything. I don't do drugs." Unfortunately my knees chose that moment to buckle and I turned over on one heel. I started to laugh uncontrollably, finding the whole situation hysterical. I took a deep breath and continued. "And don't change the topic. I'm mad at you....you...Barbarian!"

"What are you talking about?" Nash frowned.

"Oh, no. Don't pretend you don't know." I poked him in the chest with my finger. "Your little stunt with the bowl of stew, making me yours. No one would dance with me. You ruined my night out."

I could see the little light go off behind his eyes as he thought about what he had done and the consequences. "I'm sorry. I wasn't thinking. I just wanted to make sure you were safe."

"Safe? Ha!" I pushed at him again, hitting my hand against his chest. "Using some secret werewolf code to mark me like I was a tree." I stumbled toward him. "Oh boy." I grabbed my head. "Oh, the whole world's spinning."

Nash held me by the arms again, looking at me with concern on his face. "What did you take? You're high. Did someone give you something?"

"I am not high!"

"Nash," Holly interrupted, "Harry's just had a little too much, you know?" She looked at him, raising her eyebrows as if he *would* know what she was talking about. "We need to get her home."

Nash frowned and looked at me. "Yeah, of course." He grabbed me by the elbow again. "Come on. I'll take you home."

I pulled away. "I can walk." I took a few steps then stumbled again. Nash took my hand and, dipping his shoulder like a line backer, proceeded to pull me towards him, scooping me up and throwing me over his shoulder, fireman style.

"Hey!" I tried to lift my head, but didn't really succeed. "Whoa, the whole room is spinning." Nash shifted me on his shoulder and set off down the long hallway, Tess and Holly following behind, snickering as they went. I knew I wouldn't hear the end of this.

We came out a door at the side of the building. The chilly night air did wonders to clear my head. I certainly didn't need Nash carrying me like a sack of potatoes, even if it was giving me a great view of his fine ass.

"Hey! Put me down."

Nash let out an exasperated breath. "Suit yourself." He bent and set me on my feet, holding me while I got my legs under me. We stood for a moment, his arms wrapped around me. My eyes met his and he took a deep breath.

"Ahem." Holly cleared her throat and then giggled. "The car is this way. I'm sure we can manage on our own now, Detective."

The mood broken, I pushed away from Nash and took an uneasy step. I really wished I wasn't wearing my highest pumps at that moment. I managed to take a couple of steps without looking like a complete drunk when suddenly I was overwhelmed by a sense of dread.

"There's something wrong."

"What? Are you going to be sick?" Holly looked at me with concern.

"No, it's not me. There's something out there, something very wrong." Feeling completely sober now, I looked around the darkened street. "Can't you feel it?"

Nash and Tess both tensed, looking warily in both directions.

"No. There's nothing – "

Tess was interrupted by a shriek of fear coming from around the corner of the building ahead of us. We ran towards the sound. When we rounded the building, we stopped in shock. Nash stepped in front of me momentarily blocking my view and growled, "Stay back."

The alpha male routine was really pissing me off, but I was too shocked by what I saw to say anything. The street was in chaos. Halfway up the block, there looked to be an ongoing mob attack. Several bodies were lying on the ground in what appeared to be pieces, limbs torn off. At the centre of the mob a man fought for his life. Off to the side, a woman was swinging at several others with what looked like a piece of rebar. Further along the street, two men were locked in brutal combat, one was a werewolf judging from his speed and strength, the other looked eerily familiar.

"Are those...?" Tess's voice trailed off in disbelief.

"Zombies." I shook my head. It couldn't be true, but it was. They were in various stages of decomposition, their skin ashen grey, their clothes torn and tattered. They moved mindlessly, following the single imperative of the one who called them from the grave, scratching and clawing at anything in their way. While the sight of something I had only ever read about was chilling, it was the man engaged in deadly battle with the werewolf that shook me to the core. "That's the jack, the one from the video."

The woman was still screaming incoherently. When she saw us, she slipped and let down her guard and the zombie closest to her grabbed her, clawing at her, opening a new wound.

Nash ran forward and pulled out his gun, taking aim. His shot took the zombie in the centre of its head, its skull exploding outwards, but to no effect. "Shit!" he exclaimed, holstering his gun and running into the fray.

"Hurry, go get reinforcements," I yelled to Holly, pushing her back the way we had come. I grabbed Tess's arm and pulled her forward. "Come on. We've got to help." There was a pile of construction rubbish at the mouth of an alley. I grabbed another piece of rebar and ran towards the fight.

Zombies are mindless, feel no pain, have no heartbeat, magically animated killing machines. They don't stop unless they can no longer move. You can't shoot them or stab them, well, you can, it just won't do you much good. The only thing that stops them, is taking their legs out from under them. So that's what I did. I ran towards the mob, swinging the rebar like a golf club. The first zombie I came to went down like a bowling pin when I hacked its legs out from under it. The only problem was it just got up again. Okay, so I hadn't completely thought my game plan through. At least knocking them off their feet was slowing them down.

The male wolf that was under siege, quickly came up with his own game plan. As soon as Tess or I knocked a zombie down, he would pounce on them and using his extraordinary strength, tear their arms off. Gross, but effective. The armless zombies were left thrashing on the ground, unable to get back up.

We were making good headway through the mob, slowly moving towards the woman and Nash. When he saw that we had things under control, he moved towards the other male werewolf and the jack. Unlike the zombies, the jack moved with supernatural speed. No shambling, mindless puppet, instead it was a deadly automaton with super human strength. The jack felt no pain and whoever piloted it had total control. He also seemed to have a fair knowledge of hand-to-hand combat. As Nash approached, the jack pinned the male wolf in a choke hold. With a horrifying crack he broke the man's neck and then tossed his body aside like a rag doll.

Nash moved in on the jack, once again pulling his gun. He fired again and again, emptying the entire clip, hitting the jack in its centre mass, but it did nothing to stop it. The jack closed in and they began to fight in earnest. They grappled, seemingly matched in strength and skill. Nash took a heavy blow and went down momentarily and I caught my breath.

"Harry! Look out!" Tess's shout brought my attention back to the fight at hand. More zombies were closing in.

"Where are they all coming from?"

The woman we had been defending cowered behind Tess, sobbing hysterically and bleeding from several wounds. Tess swung her rebar club, taking out another of the shambling monsters.

"I don't know. We need those reinforcements." I hacked at the zombie stumbling towards me.

Suddenly, one of the downed yet still armed zombies grabbed Tess's foot and she fell. Sensing easy prey, the zombies shuffled towards her. "Oh shit! Harry!" Unable to use the rebar to her advantage from down on the ground, Tess began punching and kicking.

"Tess! Hold on." I tried to battle my way to her, but there were too many zombies in the way. Tess screamed in pain.

"No!" My vision went red in anger for a moment and a zombie used the opportunity to grab my arm, wrenching it backwards, its fingernails scoring marks down my bare skin. "Enough!" I screamed it at the top of my lungs, putting every ounce of energy I had and every bit of anger I felt into it.

A wave of power pulsed out from me and the zombies toppled like dominoes, turning to dust and blowing away as they hit the ground. The silence that ensued around us was almost deafening.

Nash stood, bruised and bloodied, over the now inanimate corpse of the jack. "What the hell just happened?"

"I don't know." I shook my head and looked around. I spotted Tess lying on the ground, holding her stomach. "Tess!" She was bleeding from a deep gash in her side. "Tess, are you okay?"

I tore the sleeve off the shirt of the stunned werewolf standing next to me and rushed to Tess's side. My hands trembled as I pressed the piece of cloth up against her wound, trying to stem the flow of blood.

"Harry! Tess!" Holly came running around the corner with several large werewolves and Dev, Nash's partner.

"Holly, hurry! Tess is hurt."

Holly ran to us and knelt down beside Tess. "Hold on. I can help." She pulled my hands away. "It's okay Harry, step away. Let me work."

I moved back, giving Holly room. My whole body began to tremble as the adrenaline rush subsided. A warm hand rested on my shoulder and Nash pulled me close, wrapping his jacket around me.

"Are you okay? Are you hurt?" He looked at me with concern.

I looked at my arm. It was scratched and bleeding, but other than that I was unhurt. "No, I'm okay." I held up my arm. "Just a scratch."

Dev approached, shaking his head. "What the hell happened here?" He pointed to the dead werewolf. "We've got one man down, George Wilks, according to his ID. Another man, hell, he's dead, but he looks like he's been dead a while. Strangest thing, he's full of bullet holes but there's no blood."

"Cut off his head." I pushed away from Nash to look at the corpse of the poor man that had been killed to create the jack. "You have to cut off his head. For all we know, they can still reanimate him otherwise."

"She's right," replied Nash. "We're going to need a cleaning crew to take care of this one." Nash pulled out his phone and punched a button. He stepped away from me but I could still hear what he was saying. "Yeah, it's Nash. Tell Salvador we've got a situation here behind The Lodge. We're going to need a crew."

I was swaying on my feet now that the adrenaline had left me. The burst of energy that pulsed out of me, whatever the hell it was, was also taking its toll. I turned to see Holly helping Tess to her feet.

When she noticed my attention, Tess smiled weakly. "I'm okay Harry. Nothing a little werewolf speed healing won't take care of overnight."

Relieved, I pulled Nash's jacket around me. It smelled like him, which for some reason felt comforting. A couple of Holly's reinforcements had joined us and were helping the werewolf couple that had been under attack. The woman sobbed quietly as they led them away, back towards The Lodge.

The rest of the night was mostly a blur. I can remember being led away and someone driving the three of us home. I was still wearing Nash's jacket, but he had stayed behind with Dev to see to the aftermath.

Back at the firehall, the three of us retreated to our bathrooms to clean off the blood and gore. Yay for on demand hot water!

After I scrubbed myself clean and disinfected the scratch on my arm, I stood under the blasting hot water, drifting in and out of consciousness from sheer exhaustion. I don't know how long I stood there, when I heard voices.

"Harry? Harry, are you all right?"

I don't even remember falling, but I was sitting under the shower spray when Holly found me.

"Harry!" She turned off the water and wrapped me in a towel. There were sounds of a muted argument then warm, strong arms lifted me up and carried me to my bed. I could barely keep my eyes open; I felt so tired and weak. I crawled under my covers feeling consciousness slip away. The bed dipped and someone slipped in beside me. I was too far gone to wonder what was going on, as arms wrapped around me and I was enveloped in a familiar comforting scent.

Chapter Thirteen

I woke the next morning wrapped around my favourite fluffy pillow, roused by the smell of bacon. Cocooned as I was under the covers, I contemplated just staying put, but hunger soon won out.

I crawled out of bed with a niggling feeling that I was forgetting something important that happened last night, but I drew a blank. Unfortunately, I definitely remembered the horror of our encounter with the zombies. Whoever that was on Bryce's video, he was doing serious dark magic. Although the zombies were poorly constructed, a sign that the practitioner wasn't powerful enough to call a fully formed zombie, the number that he had created and controlled was surprising. To have called that many zombies from their graves meant that he must have been augmenting his power. The only way it would have been possible that I had ever read about, was through blood magic. That meant more people had already died to lend power to his evil plans. But why? To what end? The thought was chilling.

I dressed quickly, pulling on some yoga pants and a t-shirt and headed downstairs, following the scent of bacon. Chilling thoughts and solving mysteries could wait until after breakfast.

Holly was cooking up a storm in the kitchen. She was just lifting some bacon out of the pan to drain on a paper towel when I entered the room. I was happy to see Tess sitting up at the kitchen island, scarfing down breakfast.

"Harry, you're up, just in time to get something to eat." Holly turned and held up a plate of pancakes. "Can I offer you some more, Detective?"

Nash shook his head. "No, that was great. Thanks."

I stopped short in surprise. What was he doing here? Maybe he was checking up on Tess. I tried to wipe the scowl from my face.

"Detective Nash." I nodded at Nash then turned my attention to Tess. "Tess, how are you doing?" I went to my friend and hugged her.

"I'm fine Harry. How are you?" Tess looked at me curiously.

"I'm fine. Actually, I'm great. I feel fantastic." And I did. I must have had a really good sleep because I felt totally recharged. Surprising, after how I felt the night before.

Holly and Tess were looking at me strangely. "What?" I asked. "I feel great. Honestly." My stomach growled loudly. "But not for much longer if you don't feed me. I'm starving."

Holly put a plate heaped with bacon, pancakes and eggs in front of me. "And everything is okay after last night?"

I frowned at her. "Well, no, of course not. Last night was awful. Why are you acting so weird?"

"So you don't remember anything *after* the zombies?" Holly persisted.

"No, not really." I shrugged. "I don't even remember getting out of the shower and going to bed. I guess I should thank you for saving me from drowning."

Nash pushed his stool out and stood up. "I should get going." He grabbed his jacket from the back of the chair where I had dropped it the night before. A familiar scent wafted out, tickling my memory again, but still it eluded me.

I mumbled a goodbye over a mouthful of pancakes. Holly glared at me and then came out from around the kitchen island to show Nash to the door.

"Thank you so much for everything, Detective." She clasped his hand. "You were a real life saver."

When the door had closed behind Nash, I scowled at her. "Thank you so much, Detective. You were a real life saver, Detective." I made a face. "Geez Holly, suck up much?"

Holly snapped at me with a tea towel. "Don't be a bitch, Harry. He did more than you know to help out last night."

"Was that before or after he marked me as his property?"

"I'm sure he did what he thought he had to do."

I scowled at her again. Why was she suddenly taking his side? I looked closely at her. "Oh. My. God! Did you? And he?" I gaped at Holly. No wonder Nash was still here this morning. "You slept with Nash?"

Tess laughed out loud, spraying her juice. Holly scowled at her then turned and pointed a finger at me. "No, I did not. And you had better leave it at that or you may be forced to think about things you have steadfastly tried to ignore." She wiped her hands on her apron then untied it and placed it on the counter. "I have to get ready to go to work. We're doing outreach with the homeless this afternoon."

After Holly stalked off, I turned to Tess and said, "What's her problem?"

Tess snorted a little laugh then replied, "You really don't remember anything after we got home last night?"

"Just you and Holly arguing about something and then helping me to bed. Why? What should I remember?"

Tess stood and grabbed her plate, carrying it to the sink. "Nothing." She was clearly evading the question. "Look, I've got to get to work too. It's your turn to do the dishes." She paused on her way out the door. "Oh, and there is something wrong with the computer. Do you know anything about that?"

***

Something was wrong with the computer? That was an understatement. Of course, I hadn't exactly had time to explain to Tess or Holly where Bryce had decided to take up residence. That's if he was even still there. The monitor, when I tried firing up the computer, remained black.

"Damn it, Bryce!" I gave the side of the unit a whack. "What have you done to my computer?"

HEY! STOP THAT!

"Bryce! You're still there!"

OF COURSE I'M HERE. WHERE ELSE WOULD I BE?

"I'm still thinking the whole go-to-the-light thing should be an option."

ARE YOU KIDDING? THIS IS WAY BETTER. AT LEAST IT WILL BE SOON.

I didn't particularly like the sound of that. "What do you mean, it will be soon?"

I TOLD YOU. YOUR COMPUTER IS IN SERIOUS NEED OF AN UPGRADE. BUT DON'T WORRY. I'VE TAKEN CARE OF IT.

I *really* didn't like the sound of that. "You've taken care of what?"

RELAX. I HAVE IT ALL UNDER CONTROL. JUST LET THE NERD HERD GUY IN WHEN HE GETS HERE. HIS GPS IS SHOWING HE'S FIVE MINUTES AWAY.

"Nerd Herd? You hired a computer nerd?"

JUST TO DO THE INSTALLATIONS. NO HANDS, REMEMBER?

This was getting crazier by the minute. "Installations? Of what? What is this going to cost me?"

I TOLD YOU. I HAVE IT ALL UNDER CONTROL. I'M PAYING FOR ALL THE UPGRADES.

"You're dead Bryce. You don't have any money anymore."

THE OFFSHORE BANK ACCOUNT I HAVE BEGS TO DIFFER.

An offshore bank account, working for the Cimmerian...Boy, Gran sure knew how to pick'em. Before I could question Bryce further, the door buzzer rang. As Bryce predicted, it was a guy dressed in khakis and a polo shirt announcing he was part of the Nerd Herd, the tech support for a local electronics chain. His name tag said 'Hi, My Name is Arnold'.

"Yeah, I have a delivery for A. Turing?" A. Turing as in Alan Turing, the genius mathematician? Very funny Bryce.

"Sure, I guess that's me, or uh, my brother." I stood back to let Arnold in the door. He was loaded down with several bags.

"Okay, sure. Yeah." The poor guy seemed to be living up to the whole 'doesn't interact well with women' stereotype. "There's a bunch more down in the van."

"More?"

"Uh, yeah." He nervously pushed his glasses up the bridge of his nose. "I should, uh, I should go get them."

"Okay, you do that."

As soon as Arnold left, I stomped over to the computer. "What the hell Bryce? What do you expect me to do with all this stuff?"

DON'T WORRY. THE NERD WILL TAKE CARE OF EVERYTHING.

The screen flicked from DOS-prompt black to the standard desktop. Arnold came clomping in the open door laden down with several more packages.

"I, um, I'll just leave the peripherals in the van until we're ready for them." He stood nervously.

"Sure Arnold." The poor guy started like a spooked deer at the sound of his own name. "Did my *brother* leave any instructions about what he wanted done with all this stuff?"

"Oh sure, I've got it all here on the work order." Relieved to be back in familiar territory, Arnold brandished his tablet phone.

"Okay, good. I'll leave you to it then."

Chapter Fourteen

I was having a bad case of *déjà vu*. I was once again in my room, rooting through my closet looking for something to wear. What *do* you wear to have dinner with the most powerful vampire in the city? For some reason I didn't think the style and fashion pages cover scenarios like this.

The only difference this time around, was that instead of torpedoing everything I chose, Gran was berating me for even thinking of going.

"I *have* to go Gran. I made a deal with Salvador."

"A deal with the devil more like." Gran's tone of voice, spoke volumes about how she felt about my deal. "I thought I raised you to be smarter than that."

"How about this?" Tess came into my room interrupting my reply to Gran. She held up a classy, black evening dress. "I got it on sale, but the skirt is way too long for me and I never got around to having it altered."

I grabbed the dress, glad to have an excuse to ignore Gran. It was a sleeveless, satin sheath, with a plunging v-neck. The floor length skirt had a very high slit up the side. It was the perfect length for me, on Tess it would have been about 6 inches too long.

"Tess, it's perfect."

"It shows off too much skin," Gran complained. "You walk into the devil's lair flashing that much skin, it's going to be you on the menu. You mark my words."

The door buzzer sounded below. "Who could that be?" I glanced at the clock. I would have to leave soon or I would be late. "Could you get it Tess, while I finish getting dressed?"

When I went downstairs a few minutes later after finally telling Gran to just butt out - I was in this predicament because of her in the first place - a man dressed in a chauffeur's uniform waited with Tess.

"What's going on?"

"It appears your ride to the ball is taken care of, Cinderella," Tess joked.

"Good evening, Miss Russo. Mr. Arroyo has sent me to pick you up." The chauffeur gave a little bow. "I'm Henry." He held out a long flat box. "Mr. Arroyo also sent this, with his compliments."

"Oh goody! Presents!" Tess clapped her hands and bounced up and down in exaggerated glee. "Open it! Open it!"

I took the box from Henry with some trepidation and set it on the table. The white box was tied with a red ribbon that reminded me of blood. Inside, beneath folds of more blood red tissue paper was the most gorgeous dress I have ever seen.

"Omigod! The tag says it's an Alexander McQueen." Tess didn't have to exaggerate her excitement now.

I pulled the gown out of the box. It was a bustier dress in floor length silk chiffon. The fabric was exquisitely patterned in shades of grey and charcoal. The waist was belted with a delicate silver chain. Of course, it was in my size.

"That dress must have cost a fortune." Tess reached out to touch the soft fabric.

I noticed a card at the bottom of the box. It read, "*Looking forward to our time together this evening*" and was signed "*Regards, Salvador*".

I tossed the card back into the box then gathered the dress up and placed it back inside as well.

"What are you doing?" Tess grabbed the lid of the box from my hands. "You're not going to wear it?"

"No," I replied, grabbing the lid back. "I'm already dressed and I certainly don't need Salvador Arroyo telling me what to wear like I am one of his bimbos." I turned to Henry and handed him the box. "Thank you Henry, but I won't be accepting this. You can wait in the car. I'll be down in a few minutes."

Henry bowed, his face betraying nothing. "Very well, Miss."

After Henry had left, Tess turned to me, a worried look on her face. "Are you sure about this Harry?"

"No, of course I'm not. But what other choice do we have? We'll lose our home if I don't keep my end of the deal."

"It's not going to do anyone much good if you're dead."

"Salvador isn't going to kill me. If he wanted me dead, he would have done it already."

Chapter Fifteen

It's funny how your perspective changes when someone has their hands wrapped around your throat. Turns out that maybe Salvador did want me dead. Or at least, Tomas did, and Salvador wasn't going to lift a finger to stop him.

The plan of going to the club, having a quick meal - with me not on the menu - and then getting the hell out of there, began to go sideways the moment I arrived at Dante's. Instead of going upstairs to Salvador's private balcony, Stefan, the vampire that met me at the limo, showed me through a door that led down below the club.

The basement of the club was a warren of dark, narrow hallways lined with doors behind which, who knew what was happening. Unfortunately the throbbing beat from the dance floor above wasn't enough to drown out some of the sounds filtering through the odd door, so I had a pretty good idea of what was going on behind at least some of them.

A door abruptly opened as we were walking past and I caught a glimpse inside, confirming my suspicions. We were in an S&M sex club. A few steps later, another door opened and a tall, blonde vampire wearing 5-inch, lace up platform ankle boots stepped out into the hall. She pulled a gauzy robe on over her black, patent leather corset.

"Now you be a *very* good boy Murray and wait there for me." She tapped the end of a riding crop against her black leather glove. "You know what happens when you are naughty." She turned and saw me, raising an appraising eyebrow. "Come to play,

Kitten?" she purred, reaching out with the end of the riding crop to stroke my cheek.

I flinched away, not wanting it to touch me and she laughed. I turned and looked her in the eye and it was her turn to flinch. "Not unless you want me to snap that thing in half and stake you through the heart with it, *Sweetheart.*" I smiled sweetly and her eyes widened in surprise. Her face twisted into a snarl and she took a step towards me.

Stefan put a hand against her chest, giving her a little push backwards. "Not now Simeen, this one's not for you."

Simeen threw me a contemptuous look and then turned with a flourish. Her robe billowed behind her like a cape as she stalked off down the hall. The cheeks of her bare ass jiggled as she walked. It kind of ruined the whole effect.

As we continued on in the opposite direction down the hall, I peeked into the room Simeen had just vacated. Poor Murray wasn't going anywhere. Not trussed up like a Thanksgiving turkey, hanging five feet off the floor. Nor was he apt to complain. The ball gag in his mouth would see to that. About the only thing on Murray that wasn't tied up was his flaccid penis dangling loose from his prone body. Now that was something I would never be able to un-see.

Stefan led me to a set of double doors at the end of a hallway. We had taken so many turns, I lost count and was afraid that I would never be able to find my way out of the maze on my own. The muffled music was quieter in this end of the hallway though, so I figured we had crossed through the centre of the building and were now somewhere over on the far side, away from the dance floor above.

Stefan knocked and then pushed the doors open, gesturing for me to enter. The room was more brightly lit than the gloomy hallway I had just left and I stood just inside the doors, blinking as my eyes adjusted. The doors clunked shut behind me, my guide nowhere to be seen. I turned, intending to test the doors to make sure I hadn't been locked in, when a voice beckoned, "Miss Russo. Do come in."

"Call me Harry, please. Everyone does." I turned to face Salvador. He sat at the far end of the room on a small raised platform on what appeared to be a throne. It was all very surreal and it took some will power not to laugh.

I looked around the room and found that it wasn't as well lit as I thought. In the centre of the room hung two large chandeliers, which while bright, left the periphery of the room in shadows. As far as I could tell though, Salvador and I were alone.

I walked a bit self-consciously towards the dais wishing I had worn the damn McQueen. Salvador watched me as I crossed the room, his eyes calculating. I stopped a few feet before him.

"My dear Miss Russo." I didn't bother to correct him. I guess he didn't consider himself everyone. "So wonderful of you to join me, but I see you did not accept my small gift?"

"No, thank you though, but I don't feel comfortable accepting such an expensive gift. I would prefer to keep things strictly business."

"But of course, of course. It was just a mere trifle." He waved it off with his hand, but then he must have seen something in my expression, because he added, "Do you not agree?"

"A $7000 gift, a trifle? Maybe in your world, but not mine. I could buy myself a nice used truck that doesn't break down every second week for that price."

"Yes, yes, I see. It's all a matter of perspective, isn't it?" Salvador smiled. "I would certainly like to get your perspective on last night's disturbing events." He clasped his hands in his lap, his index fingers tapping together. "What do you think happened last night?"

"What do *I* think happened?" Why was he asking my opinion when he already knew what had happened? I was sure Nash had filled him in by now. And why was I standing in his audience chamber? I thought we were going to eat dinner. Instead of voicing all those questions, I said, "Well, it's obviously connected to Bryce's video. The same practitioner that created the jack must have somehow called the zombies."

Salvador waved me off impatiently. "Yes, yes. That is clear. But what *happened* to the zombies? Why did they all disappear?"

"I don't know," I replied, shrugging. "Maybe the spell wore off? Or they were called back?"

Salvador raised his still clasped hands to his chin and began to tap his steepled index fingers on his bottom lip, apparently deep in thought. "Hmmm, yes. Could it be that you truly don't know?"

"Don't know? Why *would* I know?" I was getting more uncomfortable by the minute and it wasn't just because I was standing in 3 inch stillettos. What the hell did he want from me?

"Or perhaps," Salvador continued on, ignoring my outburst, "you have just not come to terms with it?" He nodded and I got a sense that he was no longer talking to me.

Before I could reply, I became aware of movement behind me. My vamp radar started clanging, but it was too late to do anything. My arms were suddenly grasped and wrenched behind my back. I heard a zipping sound and something hard and plastic bit into the skin around my wrists. A hand slid up the bare skin on my arm until it circled my throat. It squeezed, cutting off my breath. Another arm wrapped around my waist and I was pulled back against a solid body. A familiar voice whispered, "Time to play."

So much for not dying this evening.

Chapter Sixteen

At Tomas's words, my eyes widened in terror. I struggled in his arms, but I was held tight.

He laughed and purred, "Mmmm yes, struggle. It will make you taste that much sweeter." He forced my head to one side, exposing my carotid then rubbed his face in my hair, inhaling deeply. "The fear smells so lovely on you." He leaned in and licked my exposed neck.

I struggled again, trying to twist my neck away from his lips, but that just made him pull me tighter against him. So close, I could feel his erection pressing into me.

"Uh, uh, uh, not for you, my dear Tomas." Salvador shook his finger at us. "Let us see what we shall see." He snapped his fingers and two more vamps stepped from the shadows, half dragging, half carrying another between them. The third vampire was dishevelled and emaciated. I had never seen a vampire in such a dire condition. His lips were dry and chapped, his skin sunken, like he hadn't had anything to eat or drink for weeks, maybe months.

Tomas pulled me off to the side of the dais while the two vamps stopped in front of Salvador, depositing their burden. The vampire stumbled but caught himself before he fell. He straightened his clothes then lifted his chin in defiance and looked at Salvador.

"My dear friend Isaac, it pains me to see you like this." Salvador looked genuinely saddened.

"Then give me what I want, old friend." The man called Isaac's voice was weak and raspy.

"Do you agree to the terms?"

Isaac turned slowly and looked at me, then turned back to Salvador. "Why do you want such a thing?"

Salvador spread his hands and shrugged. "It is the only way. Do this last thing, and if you still seek what you ask, I will grant it."

Isaac hung his head. "Very well."

Tomas ran his hand through my hair, pulling my head back painfully. "Now the fun begins. I will feast on your fear."

Despite my best efforts to stop it, my heart began to race. I didn't know what the hell they had planned for me, but it didn't sound good. I struggled in Tomas's arms, trying to wrench myself free.

Isaac turned to me, a look of regret on his face. "I'm very sorry, my dear," he said and then started towards me, his fangs bared.

"What are you doing?" I looked at Salvador. "We had a deal!"

Salvador made a clicking sound with his tongue, shaking his head. "Always so suspicious, Miss Russo. Our deal is still in play. I said you would go home and you shall, whether it is as you are now, or as a vampire, is up to you."

"What?!" I couldn't believe what I was hearing.

"You see my friend Isaac wants something most desperately and I have told him he may have it but first he must, how shall I put it? Quench his thirst. On you." He tapped his lip with his finger pensively then shook his head. "I'm afraid though, that Isaac has been starving himself for much too long. I do believe that once he starts feeding there will be no stopping him."

"You can stop him. You don't have to do this!" I struggled against Tomas. "Don't do this!" I looked at

Isaac. He was only a few steps away from me now, but he was struggling. Whether it was due to his weakened state or disgust at what he was about to do, I don't know. "Please, Isaac! Don't do this."

Isaac stopped suddenly and frowned. "I'm sorry. I truly am. But I must."

Tomas grabbed my hair again, tilting my head to expose my neck. My mind was reeling with the thought of what was about to happen. I couldn't let it happen. I had to stop it. I slammed my stiletto heel down on top of Tomas's foot. He cried out and his grip in my hair loosened. I whipped my head back, cracking it against his face then pushed myself away from him, feeling slightly dizzy. I was free, but my hands were still fastened tight behind me. I backed away quickly keeping my eyes on Isaac. He turned to follow me, his fangs glistening with what little saliva he had left, his breath rasping.

"You bitch!" Tomas held his nose. I had broken it. He lunged for me, grabbing my arm and wrenching it up painfully. He dragged me towards Isaac. "Take her before I do," he said in disgust. He pushed my head to the side again.

"Isaac! Isaac! Listen to me! Don't do this. Please, don't do this." My only hope was to try and convince him to stop.

Isaac's steps faltered. He reached out and grabbed me by my shoulders. I struggled, managing to turn my head enough to look him in the eye. "Isaac. You must not do this." I put every ounce of my will into my words. "You will not do this. My safety is your primary concern. You cannot hurt me."

Isaac's face contorted with pain. He roared in anguish then lunged. Preparing myself for the worst, I closed my eyes, only to end up on the floor in a heap. In shock, I watched while Isaac grappled with Tomas.

"Marvelous! Marvelous!" Salvador applauded. "Enough my dear friend Isaac. Enough. She is quite safe now. No harm will come to her this night. You have my word."

Isaac backed away from Tomas and fell to his knees sobbing. "No, no, no. Oh my friend, what have you done?" He looked up at Salvador. "What have you done?"

Salvador's face became serious. "What I must."

"Will somebody please tell me what the hell is going on?" I struggled to my feet, my hands still cinched behind my back. Tomas moved towards me and I backed away warily. Isaac surged to his feet.

Tomas held up his hands in surrender. "Relax, relax." He reached behind me and cut the ties on my wrists with a small knife he had concealed in his hand.

Free at last, I rubbed my raw wrists. They were scored where the flex strip had dug into my flesh during my struggles. "I mean it. What the hell just happened?"

Salvador rose from his chair, his arms open in welcome. "All in due time my dear Miss Russo, all in due time."

Isaac, who had been swaying on his feet, suddenly collapsed with a groan. He was barely showing any of the energy aura that would mark him as a vampire. "Your friend is dying," I said to Salvador. "How is that possible? What's wrong with him?"

"That is not my story to tell," Salvador replied. "He needs to feed if he is to survive." Salvador looked at me expectantly.

"What? You expect me to...?" My voice trailed off. I couldn't comprehend what he was suggesting after what had just occurred.

"You made Isaac yours. He is now your responsibility." Salvador shrugged as if it didn't matter one way or another to him.

I shook my head in denial. I didn't understand what Salvador was talking about, or at least, I didn't want to understand. But despite the fact that Isaac was practically a ravening monster a few minutes ago, I didn't want to watch him die. And, I knew what Salvador said was true. I *had* done something. I had coerced Isaac in some way to prevent him from hurting me and whatever I had done forged a connection between us, because I could feel Isaac's pain.

I moved towards Isaac warily, afraid he might jump me again.

"You are totally safe with poor Isaac now." Salvador smiled. "You made sure of that, did you not?"

I scowled at Salvador and crouched down beside Isaac. He roused, shaking his head.

"No, no, I cannot." He tried weakly to push himself away.

"You must, Isaac. You must. You have a purpose now, do you not?" Salvador stepped down from the dais and began walking towards us.

Isaac closed his eyes briefly, shaking his head. He took a ragged breath then opened his eyes and looked at me with determination. "I do not have the strength to glamour your pain away."

"It's okay. Just do it."

"I regret that I will hurt you."

"It's all right." I reached out to him, cradling his upper body and presenting my wrist to him.

After a moment's hesitation, Isaac reached for my arm, baring his fangs. There was a sharp pain as he broke through my already abraded skin and I sucked in a breath. I felt the pull of his mouth as he drank my blood, but then he pushed my arm away, a look of surprise on his face. He looked at Salvador and said, "I understand now."

Isaac turned to look at me. "I have had sufficient to sustain me long enough to find an appropriate meal."

I decided not to worry about what he meant by that because he was right, he was already looking better, his aura stronger. He gestured to my arm and the two small punctures. "Will you allow me?"

I nodded and he bent over my wrist, his tongue sliding over the wounds. They began to heal instantly. The magic of vampire spit. Yuck.

Salvador helped Isaac to his feet and embraced him. "Thank you, my friend. Thank you." He patted Isaac on the back then turned to Tomas. "Take Isaac to find a suitable meal."

I had completely forgotten about Tomas. He shot me a look filled with hate. His broken nose was already healing. If he didn't get it set it was going to be crooked. He reached out to assist Isaac but Isaac shook him off and strode stiffly out the doors. With one last menacing glance at me, Tomas followed.

Salvador turned to me, a smile wide on his face. "Alone at last," he said. If I was terrified earlier, I was scared absolutely shitless now.

Chapter Seventeen

I never would have thought that hearing there had been another zombie attack would be welcome news, but I could have kissed Nash when he barged in moments later saying just that. For the first time since meeting him, I wasn't going to complain about him showing up uninvited.

"There have been two more separate attacks," Nash spoke to Salvador, but his eyes found mine. He took a step towards me, a look of concern briefly passing over his face, but then he seemed to catch himself and stopped, turning away to face Salvador. "We're going to need to do some containment. There have been civilian casualties."

Civilian casualties. I assumed he must mean norms. We had to figure out who was doing this before even more people were hurt or killed. Salvador and Nash began making plans to handle the situation. I used the distraction to step away into the shadows to check my phone. There were six missed calls from Tess and a text message. A little excessive, but I guess I can't blame her for being worried about me. I quickly texted her back that I was okay but couldn't talk.

"Of course you will take Miss Russo with you," Salvador said, pulling me back to the conversation.

"Me?" I squeaked in surprise. "What do you need me for?" Both men turned to look at me. Nash looked grim but Salvador looked calculating.

"I only thought, Miss Russo, that perhaps your special..." Salvador paused, gesturing with his hands like he was trying to find the right words, "*talents* may prove useful." I started to protest but Salvador continued on. "Perhaps a lingering spirit you might interrogate? Provide our dear Detective Nash with some leads?"

Nash frowned but remained silent. Salvador looked at me expectantly. I rolled my eyes. "Fine, fine." I'd do almost anything just to get out of there. I looked down at my dress. "But I'm not going anywhere dressed like this."

***

I should have kept my big, fat mouth shut.

I stood outside the club dressed like that chick from Underworld, waiting for Nash, and while I was totally keeping the cool, full-length black leather duster, I could have done without the leather hot pants and bustier. When I complained and asked why there wasn't a single T-shirt or blouse available, the response was that my current get-up would be better for blending in with the others. Unfortunately, it was true. They all looked like roadies for Motley Crue or something as they piled into the black van waiting behind Nash's SUV. All except one that is, who stepped away from the van and came to stand beside me. He was elegantly dressed in a suit that looked more Tom Ford than Nikki Sixx. His dark, shoulder length hair had that freshly washed and brushed gleam, his beard neatly trimmed. He turned to look at me with familiar blue eyes.

I did a double take when I realized it was Isaac. While his eyes were still a bit sunken and his complexion sallow, he looked remarkably better, especially with his formerly scraggly beard neat and trim. He certainly looked nothing like the starved, dishevelled creature I had encountered earlier.

"Hey! Ride in the van with the rest," Nash jerked a thumb at the van as he opened the passenger door of the SUV for me.

"I must ride with Miss Russo," Isaac replied, unaffected by Nash's gruff orders.

I placed my hand on Nash's chest telling him to back off. "It's okay. He's with me." At Nash's frown, I added, "Long story."

To say the trip from Dante's to the scene of the second attack was a little chilly, would be an understatement. Nash alternated between glaring at me and glaring at Isaac in the rear-view mirror. Isaac was unfazed by Nash's behaviour. I was getting close to smacking him. Luckily, we arrived at Bacchus, another of Salvador's clubs, although this one was a little more upscale - less Goth, more bling - before any violence ensued.

The attack had taken place in an alley at the side of the club. The area was now cordoned off with yellow police tape. A black coroner's van had pulled up near the entrance to the alley, the attendants cooling their heels at the side of the van, obviously waiting for the go-ahead to clear the scene.

The clean-up crew pulled up behind us in the van and spilled out, immediately getting to work. Several of the vamps insinuated themselves into the crowd. I assumed they were on glamour patrol, tasked with adjusting the memories of any norms to jibe with whatever cover story had been concocted. I had never really thought about it before, but I wondered how many of these types of cover-ups had there been over the years? Vampire attacks made to look like muggings and that sort of thing.

I didn't have time to worry about past cover ups, as Nash strode to the mouth of the alley and held the crime scene tape up expectantly, waiting for me to duck under. I noticed he didn't extend the same courtesy to Isaac. With a little smirk, Isaac lifted the tape and ducked under as well.

The first thing I noticed was the overwhelming sense of wrong I felt. It was almost overpowering and I staggered to lean against the side of the building. There was a scuffle of boots as both Nash and Isaac rushed to my side. Upon seeing each other they stopped short, Nash glaring and Isaac looking aloof but determined. Great, now I had two alpha males dogging my heels. I frowned at both of them and stepped further into the alley.

Like the aftermath of the attack at The Lodge, the scene was something out of a nightmare, body parts strewn everywhere. Unlike the scene from the night before, there was also a lot of blood and what looked like intestines puddled near one of the victims. I turned away, trying to block out the images while a wave of nausea washed over me.

"Are you alright, Miss Russo?" Isaac's voice was quiet, almost calming.

"Harry, just call me Harry. I'm okay. I just need a minute."

"I shouldn't have brought you here." Nash's voice was rough with anger and concern. He reached for me, taking me by the arm. "You should wait in the truck."

I pulled my arm from his grasp, angry that he was treating me like a child again. "I'm fine. I don't need to be coddled. Let's just get this over with." The anger helped me to focus, the nausea gone.

The second victim was in much the same condition as the first, huge ribbons of flesh torn off his arms and back, and a gaping hole in his abdomen. He was farther down the alley from the first and from the position of his body, it looked like he had been trying to flee when he was taken down from behind. It was puzzling. The zombies we had encountered the night before wouldn't have been fast enough to catch a man intent on running for his life. They had merely overwhelmed us with sheer numbers. I looked at the carnage again, trying to piece the bodies back together.

"Do you have any witnesses to the attack? Anyone that can describe the zombies or knows how many there were?" I turned to look at Nash.

"A couple of the vamp bouncers that came running when they heard the screams. They're the ones that tore the zombies apart."

"It doesn't look like there were that many this time, and they must have been quicker?"

Nash looked at the mutilated body, nodding his head in agreement. "I'll have to check their statements, but I agree. That's what it looks like."

"But why are the zombies still here? Why didn't they turn to dust and return to their graves?" I shivered.

"What is it Miss, uh Harry?" Isaac, silent as ever, had approached me. "Do you feel something?"

"It just feels wrong. I don't know how to describe it," I replied, shrugging. "It just feels like it needs to be undone, set right."

"Yes, that's it." Isaac looked pleased. "You must set it right. Only you can."

"Me? How can I?" I stared at Isaac incredulously.

"Surely you aren't going to continue to deny the truth, even after what happened earlier tonight?" Isaac took me by the shoulders and stared down at me. "You can do this. I am proof of that."

"No! I don't know what you're talking about." I pushed Isaac away.

"Hey!" Nash stepped up to Isaac. "Just leave her alone."

"Come now Detective, you know as well as I why Salvador insisted she come here."

"Look, both of you, just give me a minute." I stalked a short distance away from them, my mind reeling. I had been in denial a long time; I really didn't want to face reality, but it was hard to ignore what was staring me right in the face. I knew I had done something, even if it was unintentional, that made the zombies disappear the other night and tonight I had compelled Isaac to prevent him from harming me. There were also the other vamps I had 'Obi-wan'd', getting them to let me into the club. Not to mention my ability to see and command ghosts. What I could do went beyond the realm of a simple medium's powers. Everything I read about what I was capable of doing led back to one thing, a necromancer. No wonder Salvador was so interested in me and why Tomas hated me. There hadn't been a reported necromancer in generations. Of course, maybe they were just better at staying under the radar than I had been. Although, since the first thing I did with my burgeoning power was flaunt it in the faces of a bunch of vampires and the Magister, it wouldn't take much for them to be better at staying hidden than me.

"Harry, I don't mean to rush you, but it will be dawn soon." Isaac had moved closer to me. "You must release the remains before the sun rises."

"I know, I know. I just don't know how." I really didn't have a clue. So far, everything I had done, had mostly been a fluke.

"You must focus your will. Think of the outcome you want then release your power and it will be so."

"Oh, is that all?" I huffed out a breath. "I'm sorry. I know you're trying to help." I moved to stand in the centre of the alley, surrounded by the torn off limbs and shredded torsos of the zombies. The vampires had done a number on them trying to stop them. I let my shields down a little and the sense of wrongness intensified. I closed my eyes and tried to relax. I could feel a tingle of residual power. Something about it just felt out of place. I decided to focus on it, to see if there was something I could do. Maybe if I could release that lingering power, things would be set right. Taking Isaac's advice, I focused on the bodies and returning the zombies to their graves. I took several deep cleansing breaths then released my will. I felt the power slip from me in an ever growing wave. It was like I was a pebble dropped into still water, the power radiating out from me in a ripple. As the wave passed over the zombies, they disintegrated into dust and blew away with the breeze.

The release of power staggered me. My knees buckled and I started to fall only to be supported by Nash who wrapped an arm around me, propping me up. I hadn't even realized he had been hovering there behind me, so intent I was on my purpose.

"What the hell?" Nash's voice was full of concern.

Isaac chuckled. "We'll have to work on your control. I don't think it was necessary to use quite as much power as you did." His face became concerned as he looked closer at me. "You are practically drained and you haven't fed at all today. You're dangerously close to running yourself empty, especially after what happened earlier this evening."

"That's the second time you mentioned something that happened earlier this evening. What the hell happened? What is it between you two?" Nash sounded angry again.

Isaac remained unaffected by Nash's outburst. "Does it really matter right now? Harry needs to recharge. She needs to feed."

Nash scooped me up in his arms but I protested. "Put me down. You're not carrying me out of here. It will attract too much attention. I can walk." Unfortunately, the world decided to spin right at that moment. I closed my eyes for a second until the feeling passed. "I mean it. Put me down."

Nash placed me gently on my feet. I swayed, but remained upright, thankfully.

"You'll never make it two steps like that." Nash frowned then huffed out a breath as if resigned to doing something unpleasant. I blinked in surprise as he grasped my face in both hands and kissed me. At first it was tentative, but then I felt the glorious, pure energy of his aura begin to pour into mine. I deepened the kiss, soaking it in hungrily. Nash groaned, but from pleasure, not pain, enjoying the kiss as much as me. He returned everything I gave him, his tongue finding mine. His warm hands slid underneath my coat to find the strip of bare skin at the small of my back. His touch electrified me.

"Damn it!" Nash swore as he broke off the kiss to answer his ringing phone. I took a steady step away from him. What the hell was I doing kissing him?

"What?" Nash growled into the phone. "Fantastic. We're wrapping up here too." He put his phone back in his pocket and looked at me, taking in the distance I had put between us. "That was Dev. The bodies of the zombies at the second attack site seem to have been dispersed as well."

"I'm not surprised," replied Isaac with a smirk. "We should get Harry home. That little top up you gave her will not last long."

I would have protested except for the fact I could already feel the energy drain setting in again. Trying to avoid eye contact with either of them, I squared my shoulders and made my way back to the SUV, my cheeks blazing.

Chapter Eighteen

I was being carried. Again. A part of me wanted to protest, but it seemed the part that was exhausted won out. I had fallen asleep on the drive home to the firehall. I was so tired I hadn't even woken up when Nash lifted me out of the truck. It wasn't until he stopped on the outside landing and began to argue with Isaac that I roused.

"There must be a key in there. How hard can it be to find a key in that tiny bag?"

"I assure you, there is no key in here." Isaac sounded amused.

"Hey, what the hell are you guys doing rummaging around in my purse?" I snatched the tiny clutch from Isaac's hands.

"The door is locked. We need your key."

"Just knock. Tess or Holly will let us in."

"There's no one home." Nash was beginning to sound exasperated.

"What time is it? Of course someone's home."

"Look, it's almost 5 a.m. They're asleep, or no one is home. Where's your goddam key?"

I frowned. Someone should be home. I thought Tess and Holly would be worried sick about me by now. "I'm a witch. I don't have a key."

I struggled in Nash's arms trying to get him to set me down. Finally he complied, setting me on my unsteady feet. I placed my palm on the door and nothing happened.

"I don't understand. The door should have unlocked."

"I believe that you have drained yourself to the point that you can't even do a simple hedge magic." Isaac looked at me, his eyes narrowed. Of course, my knees decided at that moment to give out on me again. I fell back against Nash who reached out to steady me. Isaac indicated that we should step aside. "If you will allow me?"

I shrugged, not sure what he meant to do and took a step back bumping into Nash again. Isaac slipped a small wallet from the breast pocket of his suit and knelt down in front of the lock. He pulled out two small lock picking tools.

"Seriously?" Nash sounded affronted.

Isaac shrugged. "One should always be prepared."

"Great," Nash muttered, "a vampire boy scout."

There was a soft click and the door swung open. Wow, that had been too easy. I think we really needed to get better locks. Isaac stepped aside and I staggered in the door, calling to Holly and Tess, but there was no sign of either of them. It was hard to believe they weren't up worrying about me like a couple of mother hens.

I turned to find Isaac waiting patiently outside the door. "I—"

Nash put his hand up to my lips to stop me from speaking. "You're not really going to invite the blood sucker in are you?"

I pushed his hand away. "Yes, I am. Come in Isaac."

"Are you nuts?" Nash looked at me in frustration. "He works for Salvador."

I struggled to pull off the long leather coat I was wearing. "Not anymore he doesn't." I smirked at Nash

129

as Isaac helped me with my coat like a perfect gentleman. "He works for me."

Nash grabbed me by the elbow pulling me away from Isaac. "What the hell are you talking about? What happened with Salvador tonight?"

Isaac took a step towards us giving Nash a menacing look. "You should unhand the lady."

If Nash had been in his wolf form, I'm sure his hackles would have been raised. As it was, he turned and growled at Isaac, pushing me behind him. "You keep out of this."

That was it. I'd had about enough of the alpha male crap. I pushed past Nash and Isaac and headed towards the stairs. "You can both stick a sock in it. I'm going to bed." I stopped and turned to Isaac. "We don't have a light tight room right now, but if you need it, you can use the storage room down the hall." I turned to Nash. "And as for you, you can take your alpha –"

"I'm afraid that wouldn't be a good idea," Isaac interrupted. "You really must feed."

"I wish you would quit saying that." I wrinkled my nose in distaste.

"Not saying it doesn't make it any less true and as I cannot assist you and as there is no one else here that can, we must rely on the Detective for assistance."

I frowned. I knew he was right no matter how much I didn't want it to be true. I was barely able to stand. I had expended too much energy tonight. I had never felt my aura so drained. If I didn't recharge I would probably pass out and slip into a coma. I needed to skim the energy I needed to replenish from the only one here besides me with a pulse. Being a werewolf, Nash would be able to give me more energy quicker without it really affecting his own aura.

I looked at Nash. "And I suppose this is all right with you?" In response Nash stepped up to me and scooped me up over his shoulder. "Hey!" I exclaimed in surprise.

"For once, maybe you should just shut up," Nash growled as he carried me up the stairs.

***

You know the feeling you get when you wake up all nice and refreshed and then the memory of the night before and all the stupid things you did slaps the grin right off your face? So do I.

I woke up snuggled and warm in my bed. I felt fantastic. I was still half asleep when I rolled over, my hand landing on a solid, warm body. Momentarily surprised, I slid my fingers through the downy hair, feeling the hard planes of a well-developed torso. My hand slid further down only to suddenly be caught in a vice-like grip around my wrist. I squeaked in surprise.

"Don't start anything you're not prepared to finish," the voice was rough with sleep. The hand released mine.

With a squeal, I leapt up and scrambled off the end of the bed and stared in shock at Nash, looking all warm and sleepy and completely comfortable in my bed. He grinned at me and then he raised an eyebrow, looking me up and down. With another squeal, I realized I wasn't wearing a shirt and I quickly attempted to cover my bare breasts with my arm. I scrambled back to the bed and grabbed a t-shirt, holding it in front of my chest.

"What the hell are you doing in my bed?" What *was* he doing there? We didn't...We hadn't...I frowned trying to remember everything that happened the night before.

Nash sat up, chuckling. "You mean you don't remember last night? Ouch." He feigned a wounded look then winked at me. He swung his legs out over the edge of the bed and started to push the covers off.

"Whoa! Wait just a minute." I turned away, my cheeks red. I'm not a prude, I just thought that one of us having seen the other naked already was enough. Damn werewolves and their lack of issues with nudity.

Nash laughed and stood up, pulling a pair of jeans up off the floor. He stepped into them and I snuck a peek – tell me you wouldn't have done the same – and discovered he had been wearing boxers in bed.

He walked towards me while buttoning his fly, a gleam in his eye. He backed me up against the wall and leaned in close, his mouth next to my ear. I took a long, slow breath, trying to still my racing heart. He smelled wonderful, like clean sheets and fresh grass and something a little bit earthy.

"Believe me, little minx, if we had done more than sleep in that bed last night, you'd remember." He threw me a smug grin and grabbed the shirt I had clutched against my chest and walked out the door.

"Hey!" I scrambled to find some clothes to pull on, settling on a cotton robe from the back of the door, and hurried down the hall after him. The events from last night were starting to come back to me, along with a sneaking suspicion about the night before last. Wanting to cut him off, I opted for the fire pole, beating him to the living room by a second or two. I was rewarded for my efforts by the look of surprise on his face.

"Nice trick," he said.

"Listen," I replied. "It's not that I'm not grateful, but I don't know why you seem to think you're my keeper or guardian angel or something now."

"You're welcome." Nash grabbed his coat from where it hung by the door.

"I said I was grateful. Let's just not make a habit of it."

Nash snorted. "That's fine by me."

He slammed the door behind him, leaving me wondering what the hell had just happened.

***

"There's a vampire sleeping in our storage closet." Tess looked half asleep.

An hour or so had passed and although I'd only had less than four hours sleep, I still felt amazing. Better than I had in ages. And while I knew the half loaf of peanut butter toast I had just demolished with a chocolate milk chaser had helped too, I really had a lot to thank Nash for. He had possibly saved my life or at least kept me from getting very sick. I frowned, trying to sort out my feelings about Nash.

"Hello? Earth to Harry?" Tess waved her hand in front of my face, snapping me out of my reverie. "Harry?"

"What? Oh yeah, the vampire." I grimaced. "Long story."

"Must have been." She sounded a little hurt. "Didn't you get any of my messages?"

"I'm sorry. I didn't get a chance to check them. What's wrong? And where's Holly?"

Tess's face fell and she looked close to tears. "That's just it, I don't know. She never came home last night."

"What?" I was surprised. Holly was the reliable one of the three of us. It was unlike her to not check in.

"I tried all her friends, the hospital...no one has seen her since she went to do outreach yesterday for her shift. She never reported back at the end of the day."

I hugged Tess. No wonder she was so upset. And then I went and disappeared practically all night too.

"Don't worry. We'll find her." I chewed my lip, thinking. "Maybe she went to visit someone back home?" Unlike Tess and me, Holly still had family back in the small community outside of town where we had grown up.

"I checked there too." Tess sat down at a stool at the kitchen counter. "I don't know where she could be. This isn't like her at all, especially with you going out last night to the Magister's. You know she was worried about you. She wouldn't have missed at least checking in." She looked up, a worried expression on her face. "You don't suppose she went to Dante's and..." She trailed off, unable to finish.

"No, she wouldn't have." I frowned. "At least, I don't think she would have." I rubbed her back reassuringly. "We'll find out. We'll find *her*. I promise." Now if only I knew how to keep that promise. Maybe we could get...no, forget that. I wasn't asking Nash for anything. But what would the police do? Surely I had watched enough cop shows to figure it out.

"I have an idea." I hurried over to the computer, Tess close on my heels.

"Whoa, Harry. What the hell did you do to the computer?" She looked in awe at the two new monitors, speakers, and laser printer.

"Yeah, about that, we've had a bit of an upgrade."

"No shit." Tess shook her head. "Where did you get the money for all this?"

"Would you believe a ghost and an off-shore bank account?"

***

I filled Tess in on the Bryce situation while I waited for the computer to boot up.

"Seriously? He's in the computer?" Tess looked at the computer with trepidation.

"Well, he was. I'm not sure if he is now. I guess we'll find out." I patted the side of the machine. "Hey Bryce! You in there?"

"Hey! Hands off sister!"

Tess and I both jumped as the disembodied voice came out of the speakers.

"What the...." Tess's eyes were wide with surprise.

"Bryce! You can talk." I was just as surprised. "And you sound like James Earl Jones?"

"What? You don't like? Check this out....Harry, I am... your father."

"Ew, no. I don't."

"That's just wrong." Tess shook her head again.

"Fine, then perhaps you prefer this? I am Bryce, human-cyborg relations."

"Ha ha! Yeah, that's slightly better. It's still kind of weird though."

"So does this mean we can't use the computer anymore?" Tess looked at the new set up skeptically.

"Check the bottom drawer."

Tess opened the desk drawer and pulled out three tablets. "You bought us tablets?"

"One for each of you. No shoe shopping or trolling online dating sites on me, thank you very much."

"Hey!" Tess protested.

"Okay, that's fine." I interrupted, "We need your help."

"How can I be of service, oh Obi-wan?"

"Ha ha. Very funny. You're mixing up the characters. I can't be Luke and Obi-wan. But seriously, Holly is missing. Can you help find her? Can you access security or traffic-cam footage?"

"You bet. Tell me where."

"Outside Dante's. We need to know if she went there last night. Do you think you could find footage of the club's entrance?"

"Piece of cake. I'll need a current photo of Holly." Several pictures flashed across the screen. *"Which of these looks most like her today?"* The pictures were all ones I had taken over the last year or so that had Holly in them.

"That one." Tess pointed to the second picture. "I mean, the second one."

"Okay. This might take a few minutes while I scan the footage."

"Omigod, Harry. This is so cool. We have our own talking super computer!"

"Shh! Don't say that. His ego is big enough to begin with."

"So while we are waiting, tell me about the vampire and why he is sleeping in our storage room and what the hell happened to you last night?"

I brought Tess up to speed on everything that happened in the last twelve hours or so. She sat back in her chair looking a little overwhelmed.

"So he's like your pet vampire or something?"

"No, of course not." Although I really wasn't sure what Isaac was to me. "He's more like my bodyguard now. He's under a compulsion to keep me safe."

Tess shrugged. "Well, I guess there are worse things than a vampire bodyguard, and with everything that is going on, maybe it's exactly what you need."

"Maybe, for now. It's not like I'm planning on leaving it this way though. As soon as I can figure out how, I'll un-compel him."

"I don't think that is possible." Isaac's voice startled us as he came around the corner from the hall. "You are safer with me as your pet vampire," he looked at Tess with a wry smile, and she blushed, "if you try to un-compel me, as you say, you will no longer be safe and therefore, I cannot let you do it."

"So you can't be un-compelled because that would go against what Harry has already compelled you to do?" Tess looked confused. So was I.

"Exactly. Quite the catch-22 as they say."

"I'm sorry Isaac." And I was, but then again, I wasn't. If I hadn't done what I had last night, whatever the hell I did, Isaac probably would have killed me, especially in the state he was in.

"There is nothing for you to apologize for. You and I are both victims of Salvador's games. And, truth be told, I am quite happy to be here, to once again have a purpose."

I wasn't quite sure what to say to that. Luckily, I was saved from having to reply by Bryce.

"*Good news. No sign of your friend on any of the security cameras at or near Dante's.*"

"That's a relief," Tess replied.

"But we still don't know what happened to Holly. How are we going to find her?" I ran my hands through my hair in frustration. "What about her cell phone? Can't you do what they do on all the TV shows and pinpoint where it is?"

"I might be able to track her using her phone's GPS or by triangulating her last position."

"Great. You do that while I go take a shower and get dressed." Another idea suddenly came to me. "And can you run the video again for Isaac?" I turned to look at Isaac. "I think that Salvador recognized the man behind the zombie attacks, maybe you will too."

Chapter Nineteen

It was late afternoon when we rolled up to the spot where Bryce had tracked Holly's cellphone. The black *Escalade* with darkly tinted windows looked very out of place for the neighbourhood. Tess and I jumped out, leaving Isaac to wait behind the wheel. Although he could manage the fading daylight - most vamps who were old enough and powerful enough could - he would wait in the car unless we needed him.

Isaac took the whole bodyguard thing seriously, although I guess he really had no choice in the matter. Rather than argue with him, I figured it was easier to just let him come along. Besides, he provided the sweet ride. It had been delivered to the firehall along with some of Isaac's clothes and other possessions sometime in the wee hours of the morning.

I looked around at the debris filled street. We were in a very poor part of the city near one of the more popular areas for the homeless. Holly had often come to this neighbourhood with her hospital outreach program, bringing medical care and food, so it wasn't a surprise that she had last been seen here.

I was on edge, worried about Holly and still a little blown away by the information Isaac had imparted on the drive across town. He had watched the security video and had in fact recognized the mage, as I suspected he would. Just who that mage was though, was the incredible part. According to Isaac, the mage on the video wielding the dagger was Levy DiCastro.

Every young witch learns about DiCastro. He's like the boogeyman, his name used to frighten young magic users to stay on the white side of magic. He was once a high-ranking mage on the Conclave, the ruling council of witches. The Conclave consists of thirteen very powerful witches or mages. The makeup of the council can change from year to year based on a nomination/selection process that ensures only the most powerful, white magic practitioners are accepted, but generally, once you're on the council you stay there for life or until you decide to retire. Each year, one of the thirteen members is selected to serve as the 'Hammer' or leader of all the witches and mages. Levy DiCastro once served as the Hammer until he was ejected from the Conclave for using dark magic. It was a real scandal that tore a rift through the witch community. The interesting thing is that it happened *over one hundred years ago.* That would make DiCastro over a hundred and fifty years old.

I didn't have time to worry about DiCastro right now though. Finding Holly was the priority. Tess and I made our way across the vacant lot. There were cardboard 'condos' scattered around amongst the abandoned shopping carts and the wreck of a burned out car. Most of the improvised shelters seemed to be vacant, their usual inhabitants out for the day, panhandling or dumpster diving or whatever. We had made up some sandwiches before we left home and we handed them out to anyone willing to talk to us about Holly. So far we hadn't had much luck. No one had seen her.

"Maybe we should try calling her phone?" Tess sounded as frustrated as I felt.

"I guess it's worth a shot, but Bryce said it seemed to be turned off now." I tried Holly's number. It rang once then went to voicemail.

"Hello? Hello? Can't talk now. Busy. Very busy."

I looked around. The speaker was an older woman pushing a laden shopping cart along the sidewalk. She was dressed in rags on top of rags with a horrible looking curly, red wig sitting on her head like a hat. She looked like a nightmare version of Lucy from the old TV shows. She held something to her ear and spoke into it and then shook it like it was broken, before putting it back to her ear.

"Hello? Can't talk. Can't talk. Busy, busy." She spoke into the phone again.

"Excuse me?" I approached the woman I was now thinking of as Lucy slowly, not wanting to spook her. "Can you help me?"

"Busy! Busy, busy, busy." She stuck whatever it was she was speaking to into the pocket of the worn housecoat she wore and started pushing her cart faster. "No time. No time."

"Wait! Do you want a sandwich?"

The cart came to a halt.

"What kind of sammich?" She bounced on her feet, anxious, ready to make her escape if necessary.

I rooted through the grocery bag. "We have ham, peanut butter, tuna."

"No cat food. No cat food." She started to push her cart again.

"Wait! Okay, no tuna. How about some nice ham? Or peanut butter and jelly?"

She stopped her cart again. "What kind of jelly?"

"Strawberry." I hoped it was the right answer.

"Strawberry. Strawberry is good. Don't like no grape. The 'J' should be strawberry. PBJ is peanut butter and strawberry."

"Well I have..." I looked in the bag, "two of them. All yours, if you can take a minute from your busy schedule and talk to me."

Lucy grimaced, clearly thinking about it. "Okay. Okay. But don't touch my cart. No one touches my cart."

"It's okay. We," I indicated to Tess and myself, "we won't touch anything." I held out the sandwiches. Lucy hesitantly let go of her cart then scuttled over to snatch them from my hand. For a minute I thought she was going to just take them and run, but she shuffled a few steps away, out of reach. She hastily tore the plastic wrap off one of the sandwiches, stuffing half of it in her mouth.

Tess made a bit of a face and whispered, "We should have brought some milk. She'll never be able to talk after that mouthful."

I snorted a little laugh and then tried to cover it by clearing my throat. "Ma'am, I was wondering if you could look at this picture and tell me if you have seen this woman in the last day or so?" I held up a picture of Holly on my phone for her to see.

Lucy squinted at the picture and then her eyes went wide. She hastily stuffed the rest of the sandwich into her pocket and started to run back to her cart. "No, no, no! All gone. All gone. Not here." She started pushing her cart along the sidewalk. "No talk. All gone."

"Hey!" Tess shouted after her.

"Wait! What's wrong?" I stuffed my phone in my pocket and Tess and I hurried after her.

She pushed her cart around the corner and into the mouth of an alley. Tess caught up to her and grabbed for her cart to stop her.

"DON'T TOUCH MY STUFF!" Lucy yelled at the top of her lungs and pulled what looked to be a plastic picnic knife out of her pocket, waving it threateningly.

Tess threw her hands up in surrender. "Alright, alright. Sorry."

"Please," I said. "We just want to find our friend."

"All gone. Gone away. Hope she not come back." Lucy shook her head, but she was looking off into the distance down the alley.

I followed her gaze, puzzled by what I saw. I walked a little further into the alley. The sun had almost set so it was filled with shadows making it hard to see anything, but there was one pocket of shadow where I could see furtive movements.

"Why would you say that about our friend?" Tess asked Lucy. "Of course we want her to come back."

"No, not come back." Lucy shook her head. "Not good. Not come back."

I looked at Lucy. Her eyes seemed to be tracking the same movements I could see. After a moment, she noticed that I was watching. "Do you see? You see?" She gestured down the alley to where I could see the diaphanous outline of a spirit. It was a man, dressed in a ragged suit, wearing a rumpled old fedora. He paced back and forth muttering to himself. There wouldn't be much use in trying to talk to him though. I'd seen this type of ghost before. I don't know what they are really called, or if there's actually a name for them, but I call them 'repeaters', ghosts that just repeat the same familiar action over and over, oblivious to anything else around them.

"Yes, I can see him," I said to Lucy.

She looked at me with astonishment. "You see. He go. Go, go, go. Had to go." She pointed at the spirit. "Not good. He come back. Not good."

"What do you mean? Where did he go?"

"All gone. All, all gone. Others go. Not come back."

This wasn't getting us anywhere. Obviously Lucy had a bit of the gift. She could see the ghost, but what did she mean about having to go? I wanted to question her more, but just then, my phone rang.

"Hello?" I didn't recognize the number so I was surprised when Salvador's voice purred back over the line.

"My dear Miss Russo. So glad I was able to reach you." Even over the phone, his voice gave me the heebee-geebees.

"Magister, I'm kind of busy right now." I frowned looking over at Lucy. She had reached into her pocket to remove something and was talking into it. From closer up, it looked like an actual cell phone. I gestured to Tess to take a closer look.

"I'm sure you are, but whatever it is, it will have to wait. You and I have some unfinished business to discuss."

"We do?"

"Certainly," Salvador's reply sounded surprised. "We did not complete our dinner last evening so I'm afraid our deal is void."

"What?" Did he mean the deal for the firehall? As far as I was concerned I had held up my end of the bargain. "Wait a minute. I arrived for dinner last night as promised."

"But we never ate dinner."

"That's not my fault." Damn vampires and their loopholes.

"Nevertheless," Salvador continued, "the terms will need to be renegotiated and as such, I require your presence this evening. Say around ten?" Before I could answer, he hung up, leaving me staring at my phone.

"Mine!" Lucy clutched at the phone in her hand. "Mine, mine, mine."

"Yes, it's yours." Tess held up her hands trying to placate Lucy. "I just want to see it. You can still hold it. Just hold it up so I can see it."

Lucy warily held up the phone. It was a smartphone in a hot pink case. The screen had been smashed like someone had stepped on it. Tess and I exchanged a glance.

"Can I see the back of your phone?" I asked Lucy, cautiously coming to stand a little closer.

Lucy flipped the phone over, holding it and gesturing like she was Vanna White. "My phone. Mine."

"Yes. It's a lovely phone." It was. Only it used to be Holly's. "Where did you get it?"

Lucy's face became totally shut down. She didn't want to talk to us anymore. "No. No, no, no."

Tess huffed out a breath in frustration. "This is getting us nowhere."

"Ladies," Isaac's voice startled us, "sorry to interrupt." Lucy froze, like a deer caught in the headlights.

"Geez Isaac. How long have you been standing there? You scared the shit out of us."

"I apologize. I sensed a change in your emotions, you're upset."

"You sensed?" What was he talking about?

145

Isaac looked a little uncomfortable. "It's a side effect of last night. I seem to be able to sense your emotions, the strong ones, at least."

"And you're just telling me this now?" Unbelievable! What else had I managed to screw up I wonder?

"Guys?" Tess interrupted, concern in her voice. "Something's wrong with..." She pointed at Lucy who appeared to be completely frozen, standing there, staring like she was a wax figure.

"Oh crap! Is she having a stroke or something?" I asked. I stepped closer to her and waved my hand in front of her unblinking eyes.

"I'm afraid that's my fault as well," Isaac replied. "I didn't want to frighten her further."

"You can do that? Just freeze her in place like that?" Tess was aghast.

"Using glamour, yes." Isaac shrugged like it was no big deal. I suppose to him, it wasn't, especially for someone that hunted humans for dinner.

"But how is that going to help us?" I wondered aloud.

"I can try and read her memories of the last day," Isaac answered matter-of-factly, as if it was a normal occurrence.

"Will it hurt her?" I frowned. I really wanted to know what Lucy was babbling about, but I didn't want to do anything to damage her any further than she already seemed to be.

"Not to worry. She will feel nothing and will be unaware it happened."

"In that case, do it. Please," I added, hopefully making it a request rather than an order.

Isaac approached Lucy, a look of compassion on his face. He placed his hands on either side of her head, at her temples. "Be at peace, little sister. Close your eyes." Lucy's eyes fluttered closed. "Think back to yesterday when you saw Holly. You remember Holly." Lucy started to nod. "Yes, that's right. Just think back to when you last saw Holly."

A few minutes later, Lucy, whose name turned out to be Joanne, was on her way back down the alley with the entire bag of sandwiches hidden in her cart. Isaac had learned everything we needed to know. Unfortunately, it wasn't good. Joanne had seen Holly yesterday, right before a familiar white van arrived to round up more of the homeless. The men in the van had been to the area before, promising jobs, beds and food. They had taken a van load, including our friend the pacing ghost. None of the men or women that went with the men in the van ever returned, but Joanne had seen several of their spirits lingering in the area, including the pacing man. When the van had arrived yesterday, Holly and her outreach partner, Oksana, questioned the men. The men had gotten angry and forced both Oksana and Holly and everyone else already in the van to go with them at gunpoint. During the scuffle, Holly's phone had been thrown to the ground and one of the men had stomped on it. Joanne picked it up after the van had pulled away.

"What could they want with them?" Tess asked.

Isaac shook his head. "Joanne did not have that information."

I was getting a sick feeling in the pit of my stomach. "I have a very bad feeling about this. We need to get home."

"Why? What are you thinking?" Tess asked anxiously. I shook my head. I didn't want to put words to my suspicions until I checked something out.

Chapter Twenty

"We have to find her!" Tess paced the floor.

My suspicions, unfortunately, proved right. When we arrived back at the firehall, I went straight to the computer and asked Bryce to replay the security video one more time. I watched it again with Isaac, paying close attention to the victim. The man was dressed poorly, his clothes worn. When the point came in the video when the blindfold was removed, Isaac nodded. "Yes, you are correct," he said, confirming my fears. "That is one of the men that Joanne saw being enticed into the white van."

"We have to call Nash," Tess stopped her pacing and looked at me. "People are being kidnapped right off the street and then murdered. The police will have to help us now."

"And tell them what?" I wondered. "We don't have any proof. Unless you think they will consider a vampire mind-meld with a bag lady proof?"

"That's why we have to tell Nash. He'll believe us." Tess flopped down on the sofa beside me. She put her head on my shoulder. "What if we're too late?"

"No. We can't think like that. We're not too late. We'll find her." I gave her a hug, trying not to think the worst myself. I didn't want to face the thought that Holly might already be dead, murdered to help create DiCastro's zombie army. "We just have to find DiCastro. We don't need the police when we have Bryce." As far as I was concerned, it was true. We already had Bryce searching for the van's registration in the DMV database as well as doing a property search for any buildings listed under the name DiCastro or any variant of the name.

"You just want to avoid Nash." Tess said with a scowl, folding her arms across her chest.

"So what if I do? We don't need him bossing us around," I replied belligerently. I was probably a bit harsh with Tess, mainly because I was angry at myself for the way the thought of seeing Nash again made me feel.

"Methinks the lady doth protest too much," Isaac mused.

"Shut up, you," I growled at him. I hadn't forgotten the fact that he could read my emotions, which, when it came to Nash, were a mess. I certainly didn't need Isaac interpreting them for me. I ran a hand through my hair in frustration. "Look, when we find where Holly has been taken, we'll get the police involved. Until then, I really don't think there is anything they'll do that we can't, if they even do anything at all. It hasn't been 48 hours yet. They probably wouldn't even let us file a missing persons report." I gave Tess another comforting hug. "We're going to find her," I promised.

"Okay." Tess hugged me back tightly. "I'm just really worried about her."

"I know. Me too." I took a deep breath. "Okay then. You and Bryce keep checking for real estate that could be DiCastro's. I have an errand I have to run."

"An errand? Now?"

"Yeah. That phone call earlier was the Magister. I've been summoned."

Tess turned to look at Isaac. "And you're just going to let her go back there? I thought you were supposed to be looking after her safety."

Isaac cocked an eyebrow. "I am."

Tess frowned. "So what you aren't saying is that it would be more dangerous for her not to go?"

Isaac shrugged. "Salvador gets what he wants one way or another. The safer road is to not antagonize him."

"Great. Let's go and get this stupid renegotiation done then." I started to pull on my jacket.

Tess looked at me critically. "You're going to go see him like that?"

"What's wrong with what I have on?" I wore my favourite boot cut jeans, a t-shirt and hoodie. I had wrapped a fringed scarf around my neck and was pulling on my light brown, bomber style leather jacket to keep away the cold. The evening air can be pretty nippy here in mid-October. "I'm done with dressing up for him."

***

I know what you are going to think. I should just stop making statements like that, the kind that tempt fate. Why else would I find myself dressed in that same Alexander McQueen dress that I had turned down the night before? I admit it was getting a little tiresome to have to keep eating my words. But I'm getting ahead of myself.

When we arrived at Dante's, Isaac and I were shown upstairs to the balcony overlooking the club. Salvador was already there and when we entered the room he waved his hand and the vampires and other hangers-on slunk away leaving us alone with him.

"My dear Miss Russo, Isaac. Come in, come in." Salvador smiled and patted the seat beside him. "Please my dear, have a seat."

After a slight hesitation, I sat down on the seat Salvador had indicated, trying to maintain as much distance between us as possible. Isaac took up watch, standing behind me.

"Magister," I said by way of greeting.

"Please, Salvador, you must call me Salvador. And I will call you Angharad. Afterall, we will be seeing so much more of each other in the future." He gestured and the waiter came over with a bottle of champagne. He poured two glasses then retreated out of sight again.

"About that – "

"Please drink," Salvador interrupted. He handed me a champagne glass then lifted his own. *"Salut!* To our new relationship." He reached over and clinked his glass against mine.

"Our relationship?" I sat dumbfounded, my champagne untouched. "What relationship?"

"Why, our burgeoning friendship, of course," Salvador replied, feigning surprise. "A friendship that will only continue to grow at our weekly dinners over the next, shall we say, year?"

"A year! Wait a minute. The deal was one dinner. One time." I set my champagne glass down.

"Yes, however that deal is no longer on the table, as you did not live up to the terms of our agreement." Salvador held up a finger stalling my protests. "But as I said, I am willing to renegotiate the terms."

"Fine, but six months. I will meet you once a week, for dinner, for six months." I couldn't lose the firehall, if I had to eat a meal every week with Salvador for six months, so be it.

Salvador appeared to give it some thought and then smiled. "Nine months," he countered.

I chewed my lip. I'm sure most people would think I was crazy for even negotiating with the Magister. Usually, you just do what he tells you or face the consequences, but for some reason or another, Salvador was playing this game, so I'd play too. "Nine months, but if you have to cancel a dinner or I show up and for some reason dinner is interrupted, it still counts as the one for that week. If I have to cancel, I'll make it up." I thought for a moment. "And, you won't expect me to dress up like one of your bimbettes. I'll wear what I feel is appropriate."

"My bimbettes?" Salvador smiled. "Ah, yes." He looked at me pointedly. "That will not be a problem. However, I do reserve the right to present you with the occasional gift, which you will accept."

I huffed out a little breath. "Fine. Deal?"

"One more thing," Salvador added. "I will from time to time require your presence or your assistance in matters pertaining to your particular talents. This you will also do for me."

Isaac shifted position behind me. Now we were getting to what Salvador really wanted.

I thought for a moment then replied, "No." It was my turn to put up my hand to stall Salvador. "I won't negotiate when I don't know the specifics of what you might ask me to do. But, I will stipulate that I will be open to providing assistance or attending other, uh, events, as mutually agreed upon at the time. However, these will count towards my dinner date balance and I reserve the right to say no."

Salvador smiled again and sat back in his seat which only put me more on edge. My mind reeled. Did I cover all the bases? I thought I had. Hopefully I wasn't going to live to regret this deal, or worse, die because of it.

"I will accept those terms." Salvador signalled and the waiter refilled his glass. "We will drink to seal the bargain." He raised his glass and I followed suit. Salvador clinked his glass to mine and we drank. The champagne was probably the most expensive I had ever tasted, but it turned to bitter acid in my mouth with Salvador's next words.

"Now you best hurry. Simeen will see you get dressed."

"Excuse me?" I spluttered.

"You cannot attend the parley dressed like a college co-ed."

"Parley? What parley?"

"Surely you do not want to miss my meeting with Levy DiCastro?" Salvador looked at me pointedly.

And that's how I found myself being dressed and coiffed and painted like some sort of fashion model Barbie doll by an insolent Simeen, the domanatrix. My life had definitely veered off into the land of strange.

***

With one last blast of hairspray, Simeen announced I was ready. "Wow," I said when she turned the chair so I could look at myself in the mirror. I had to admit, she did a spectacular job. I hardly recognized myself. She had applied make-up in such a way that it accentuated my eyes and cheekbones, but looked like I was really wearing no make-up at all. She even managed to tame my usually tousled, short hair into something resembling a hairstyle.

She shrugged and replied with a sneer, "I could only do so much with what I had." She picked up a beautiful crystal bracelet and snapped it on my wrist. "You will wear this. Now get dressed." She turned and stalked out of the room, stopping in the doorway to add, "Wait here for your escort. Do not roam around the halls on your own." She pulled the door shut behind her, leaving me alone.

I scrambled out of my remaining clothes and pulled on the gorgeous McQueen dress. Its charcoal silk chiffon was almost weightless and floated around me like the smoke it was patterned after. The bodice had built in support so luckily I didn't have to worry about finding a strapless bra. I was just struggling to get the zipper up, when there was a knock at the door.

I shuffled across the room holding the dress together at the back so that I didn't have a wardrobe malfunction. I assumed it would be Isaac come to escort me to whatever we were calling this shindig, but when I opened the door Nash stood there, an impatient look on his face. For a moment, we both stood and looked at each other in surprise. I barely recognized him, dressed as he was in a slim-fit, dark charcoal suit. It fit him perfectly with just a hint of cuff showing at the end of each sleeve. His shirt and tie were also the same shade of charcoal and the lapels of his jacket had a satin finish, giving him a formal appearance. He looked at me with his piercing green eyes and suddenly I felt self-conscious.

"O-oh, it's you," I stammered, backing away from the door to let him in. "I guess I was expecting Isaac."

Nash stepped into the room, shutting the door behind him. "No, you're stuck with me. DiCastro knows Isaac and it would only draw his attention to you if you were seen with him."

"What's going on Nash? Why is DiCastro coming here? Why is Salvador just letting him walk in here after everything he has done?" Simeen had refused to even talk to me, let alone answer any of my questions. With Nash's arrival, I couldn't seem to keep myself from babbling them all out. "He has Holly. I'm sure of it. We shouldn't be dressing up to greet him, we should be grabbing him and getting him to tell us what he has done with all the people he's kidnapped." The worry and anger I felt were apparent in my voice.

Nash took a step towards me and reached out to me reassuringly. "I know about Holly. Tess told me what you found out. Damn vampire politics. DiCastro invoked the right to parley and Salvador granted it. There's nothing we can do to him right now. But I promise you, once it's over, all bets are off. We'll stop DiCastro and we'll do everything we can to get Holly back safely."

Nash's hand on my bare arm felt warm, making my skin tingle. We stood for a moment like that, until I remembered I was standing there with my dress unzipped. I blushed and turned my back to Nash. "Can you help me? The zipper is stuck."

Nash's fingers brushed against my bare shoulder as he pulled the zip up the last few inches. When the zipper reached the top, he dipped his head towards my neck and inhaled deeply. I jumped away, turning to look at him.

"Why do you keep sniffing me like that?" I asked

"I..." Nash look embarrassed.

"You did that when we first met too," I continued on, ignoring Nash's stammering.

Nash looked uncomfortable for a moment as if weighing whether to answer or not. Finally, he huffed out a breath and then said, "My wolf likes the way you smell."

"What?" I stepped further away from him. "I don't smell." I fought the urge to lift my arm and check.

Nash put out his hand to stop me. "That came out wrong. Of course you don't smell. I mean your scent. My wolf is attracted to your scent."

"I'm really not sure if that sounds any better." I frowned at Nash. "So your wolf is attracted to me, but not you?"

Nash ran a hand through his hair, mussing it up, which only made him look sexier. "No, it's not that. I do find you attractive. And aggravating and stubborn and – "

"Okay, okay. I get the picture." I turned away from Nash.

Nash reached out and grabbed my arm, spinning me back to face him. "No, I don't think you do." He pulled me close and looked down at me. He grasped my chin, tilting my face up to his. "If I've come across as overbearing, it's because my wolf just wants to protect you."

"I don't need – "

The rest of my sentence was lost when Nash's mouth captured mine. His hand slid down to the small of my back pulling me closer. My lips parted and his tongue found mine, kissing me deeply. He was a great kisser, teasing one minute, devouring my mouth the next. We pulled apart suddenly at the sound of a knock on the door.

"You are summoned to the audience chamber," said a muffled voice.

We stood for a moment, breathless, looking at one another. I wasn't sure what had just happened. Finally Nash held out his arm and said, "Shall we?"

I took his arm and let him escort me to whatever the hell was going to happen next.

Chapter Twenty-one

It looked more like a cocktail party, if a somewhat subdued one, than the lynch mob I wanted it to be. The audience chamber was over half-filled with vampires and a smattering of werewolves. I'm sure there were a few witches, although I couldn't identify them without truly scanning the crowd. Everyone milled about, many with wine glasses in their hands, dressed in their finery. It was a weird juxtaposition to the crowd dancing somewhere above our heads in their Goth regalia.

We entered through a side door, rather than the double doors I was familiar with. The crowd parted to let us pass, the werewolves being quicker to move out of Nash's way than the vampires. Several of the male and some female vamps stared at me appreciatively, but I didn't let it go to my head. It was probably the dress or the fact that I was the fresh meat at the party. Nash was positively bristling, his protective alpha male kicking into overdrive, by the time we neared the dais.

Salvador had been watching us from the time we were about halfway across the room. He inclined his head slightly in acknowledgement, but said nothing. Nash approached a familiar looking woman surrounded by what could only be personal bodyguards. He gave her a peck on the cheek and she in turn patted his cheek maternally. They traded a few quiet comments that I didn't catch, mainly because I didn't think it would be polite to eavesdrop. I looked around the room while I waited and spotted Isaac. Like Nash, he was dressed in a formal, excellently tailored dark suit. When our eyes met, he nodded surreptitiously and then went back to casually leaning against the wall.

"...and you look positively lovely this evening, Angharad," Eleanor said, drawing my attention back.

"Please, call me Harry," my reply automatic. "And thank you," I added uncomfortably.

"I know all this frippery must be hard for you dear, with your friend missing," Eleanor replied. I looked at Nash. Of course he would have told the Triad about what we had discovered. "But the conventions must be upheld."

I was tempted to say something about what I thought they should do with the conventions, when a familiar voice called my name.

I looked around and spotted Tess approaching. She wore her black, lace top jumpsuit which made her legs look longer than they were. It was classy and elegant and she fit right in with the rest of the crowd. I knew she had chosen it though, because it would also be easy to fight in, if she needed.

"Tess! What are you doing here?" I asked, giving her a hug.

"I'm part of your bodyguard detail," she replied with a wink. "You look amazing in that dress."

I made a face at her. "I swear Salvador made this whole parley thing up just so I'd have to wear the damn thing. I mean, a *parley*? I didn't realize that vampires held to the pirate code. I think they've watched *Pirates of the Caribbean* too many times."

Tess and I snickered together causing Nash to frown at us like a disapproving parent. Unfortunately, it only made us giggle more. A waiter passed by with a tray of drinks and I grabbed two, handing one to Tess.

"*Damn to the depths whatever man thought of parley*," I quoted. Tess and I had seen the movie a few times ourselves.

"*That would be the French,*" Tess answered and we both burst into laughter. I raised my glass to Nash and his scowl, and tossed back the wine, placing the empty glass on a passing waiter's tray. Nash looked like he was about to say something when the large double doors at the far end of the room swung open and the crowd hushed.

The moment the man stepped into the room, I was overwhelmed by what can only be described as a feeling of evil. It would have staggered me, if I hadn't been prepared for it. Levy DiCastro strode into the audience chamber like he owned the place, his disdain for everyone in the hall evident on his face. He was flanked by two large men walking several paces behind him. Even from a distance I could tell they were jacks by the black magic radiating off them. I wasn't the only one disturbed by their presence. The crowd began to murmur and shift uncomfortably.

When he reached the front of the dais, DiCastro stopped. He stood straight and tilted his chin up with a sneer.

"Salvador," he said.

Salvador hadn't moved when DiCastro first made his appearance, but instead had remained sitting nonchalantly, relaxed in his seat. When DiCastro addressed him, he slowly sat up, his eyes glittering a deadly black.

"You dare bring those abominations here?" Salvador didn't raise his voice, he didn't need to. Everyone in the room could feel the power dripping from his words.

DiCastro remained arrogantly unaffected. He shrugged and replied, "I am allowed by the rules to bring two supporters." He smiled and scanned the crowd as he continued on, "And we all know how much vampires like their rules."

Salvador waved his hand impatiently. "Yes, yes. Let us get on with this shall we?"

"Certainly," DiCastro replied.

If he said anything else, I didn't hear it because I found myself doubled over in pain. Tess grabbed my arm and hissed my name.

"Harry, what's going on?" Nash was suddenly at my side, a look of concern on his face.

"Something is wrong. Oh, shit. Something is very wrong." My head throbbed and my stomach felt like it was going to reject the wine I had just drank. I looked over at DiCastro who was still verbally sparring with Salvador. I couldn't pinpoint the source of what was making me feel this way. I scanned the crowd and saw a concerned Isaac making his way over to me.

There was a commotion at the entrance to the hall and someone began to shout that there were zombies outside the club. I could hear Salvador's voice over the crowd.

"....broken the truce. Your life is forfeit."

DiCastro answered with contempt. "Truce? I have no need of a truce. I have what I came for."

Before I could wonder what he was talking about, a new sensation overcame me. This time it was coming from the bracelet on my wrist. It had begun to pulse and glow. "No! No, no, no!" I shouted, pulling at the crystal bracelet, trying to pry it off my wrist. "Get it off, get it off!"

"What is it?" Tess's face was full of concern. She looked at the glowing bracelet in shock.

"Magic. It's magic." I continued to try and wrench the bracelet off my wrist. "It's a translocation spell. It's been activated."

"Oh my God!" Tess grabbed at the bracelet trying to tear it from my wrist.

Nash looked at us as we struggled to remove the bracelet then turned and with a roar, launched himself at DiCastro. I had just a moment to see him storm through the crowd as DiCastro winked out of existence with a laugh. There was a sharp pull on my wrist and the room went out of focus. I shouted at Tess, "The bracelet. It was Simeen." There was a sensation like the floor dropping out of the room and then nothing. Everything went black.

Chapter Twenty-two

Falling.

A cold floor.

Voices.

I struggled to open my eyes but they refused to stay open, the light too bright for my senses, the pain too great. Voices were murmuring, disturbingly familiar voices. I battled against the fog to try and stay awake.

"You did it!" a voice cried out triumphantly.

"Of course I did. Just as well since you failed to deliver on your end," a second voice replied with disdain.

"My love, I'm sorry. I...."

"I don't need excuses. Take her to the infirmary and secure her there," ordered the second voice, that I now realized was DiCastro's.

Two sets of rough hands grabbed my arms and hauled me up between them, but I was unable to support my own weight, my knees buckling. I still wasn't able to keep my eyes open against the glare of the lights, the pain like daggers stabbing my brain. The forced translocation was taking its toll. My stomach lurched and the wine I drank earlier threatened to make a reappearance. Falling to my knees, I retched the contents of my stomach on the feet of one of my captors, earning a curse and kick to the head and then all was mercifully dark again.

***

"Wakey, wakey." A hand slapped my face. "Harry, wake up."

I opened my eyes cautiously, squinting at the lights, but thankfully the pain was gone. I blinked a few times, the room slowly coming into focus. I was on a gurney of some sort, my head partly raised in a semi-reclined position. My arms were secured to the rails of the gurney with plastic zip ties.

"There you are," a familiar voice said. "Here, drink this." Holly stepped into view holding a bottle with a straw to my mouth. I automatically took a sip, tasting chocolate protein shake, before the surprise kicked in.

"Holly! You're here. You're okay."

"Of course I'm fine. I'm exactly where I want to be." Holly smirked and held the straw to my face again. "Now drink this and regain your strength. We need you in top shape."

"What?" My mind reeled as it processed what Holly had just said. "Holly?"

"Poor little Harry. What's the matter? The great wunderkind can't figure it out?" She looked at me with contempt.

"I don't understand. What's happened Holly? What has DiCastro done to you?"

"Done to me? He hasn't done anything to me, at least nothing I didn't want him to do. This is my choice. I chose to follow him. Levy is going to be the greatest power the world has ever seen and I will be right there by his side."

I shook my head in denial as what Holly said soaked in. Holly was working with DiCastro? I couldn't wrap my head around it.

"Deny it all you want Harry, that is after all what you're best at, denial. You live every day denying your true self, your gift. You're a necromancer for fuck's sake. You could have been a powerful force here in Riverton, but instead you fritter it away finding lost jewelry and making sure poor, dead Aunt Sue's cat gets fed."

"How long? How long Holly?" How long had she been a traitor in our midst?

"Two fucking years! Two years I've spent being your fucking babysitter while you planted flowers and bean sprouts, and did nothing with your gift." She began to pace around the room. "Don't tell Harry about her gift," she mimicked in a squeaky voice. "Let her come into her power on her own." Scowling, she threw the half empty bottle against the wall. "Harry, Harry, Harry! It was always about you Harry, the whole time we were growing up. And you were oblivious to it all, while everyone bent over backwards to make sure you were happy with your head in the sand. I was so sick of it. I couldn't wait to get away. Finally I did, four glorious weeks away from you and Tess and your juvenile behaviour. And that's when I met Levy."

"When you were in Egypt on your vacation," I said, as the realization came to me.

"Yes, in Egypt." Holly smiled, but it wasn't the smile of the Holly I once knew. It was a cold, calculating smile. "Levy is brilliant. He had made an extraordinary discovery and was making great plans. He just needed access to a very strong power and when I told him I knew where to find the first necromancer in generations, he was understandably grateful. We became lovers and now I will be more than his Queen, I will be his Goddess when he becomes a God." Holly's face took on a fervent expression.

"Wow, you've totally lost it." I deadpanned, shaking my head. She was definitely sounding a little cuckoo for Cocoa Puffs.

Holly's face became a cold mask of hatred. "Joke all you want Harry. We'll see how funny you think it is when Levy plunges the Dagger of Asar into your heart and sucks every last drop of your power from your lifeless body. He will become the most powerful necromancer ever known; an unstoppable force, and I will be by his side. Maybe we'll even fuck while standing over your corpse."

I blinked. Uh, okay, I so wasn't expecting to hear that. "You're totally batshit crazy," I said. "I don't care whose dagger you have, you can't just kill me and steal my gift. It doesn't work that way."

"It does if you have the Dagger of Asar, otherwise known as Osiris, and you know the ritual Isis used to bring him back from Otherworld. With the blood magic released by your death and the sacrifice of the others, we will bring Osiris back to this plane and Levy will be his avatar. He will become one with the god and his powers will be boundless. Nothing, not the Cimmerian or the Triad or the Conclave will stand in his way." Holly's eyes glowed with an intensity only seen in zealots and drug addicts jonesing for their next fix. How had she managed to hide the crazy from Tess and me all this time?

I struggled with my bonds, the plastic ties biting into my skin. I had to get out of there. I knew that Nash and Tess, not to mention Isaac and I'm sure the Magister, would be looking for me. But would they find me in time?

"And just when is this little love fest supposed to take place?" I asked Holly.

"The moon will be new tomorrow. Tess and all her mutt buddies will be at their weakest, but the God of Rebirth will be at his strongest." Holly sneered at me. "No one is coming for you. Not even that stupid mutt detective who can't seem to help sniffing around you." She crossed the room to a small fridge and opened another protein shake. "Drink this or I'll get someone to help pour it down your throat. We wouldn't want you to pass out right before Levy kills you." She thrust the bottle at me.

Who was this person in front of me? I couldn't reconcile her at all with the Holly I thought I knew. Just the idea that she had been plotting behind my back for all this time, I couldn't bring myself to believe it. It made me so angry. I could feel the anger boiling up inside of me. When she reached across to hold the straw to my lips, I managed to pull up on my hand with all my strength. The zip tie cut viciously into my wrist before it broke open and I grabbed her arm in a crushing grip. I could feel her aura on the surface of her skin. It tingled against my bare hand. I imagined taking the energy from her aura into myself, feeding my own. I know it is what I had done unconsciously with Nash, but this was the first time I had ever tried to do it on purpose. Holly let out a frightened shriek and her aura pulsed. Tomas was right. Her fear was delicious. I drew more energy to myself, feeling my own depleted stores replenishing. Holly thrashed and screamed for help but she was no match for my power-boosted strength. I could feel the life force leeching out of her and I didn't care. If I was going to stand a snowflake's chance in hell of getting out of there, I would need all the energy I could get.

The door suddenly burst open surprising me, as two of DiCastro's goons ran in to help. I let go of Holly's wrist and she fell to the floor cradling her arm. She struggled to her feet looking a bit woozy and staggered across the room to a medical chest.

"You bitch!" she screamed. She came back across the room, a syringe and a bottle of clear liquid in her hand. "Hold her still but don't touch her with your bare hands."

One of the men pulled a rather large gun from underneath his coat and held it to my forehead. Needless to say I didn't move. Holly measured a dose of something I was sure would knock me out, then plunged the needle into my neck. I screamed and then the lights went out.

Chapter Twenty-three

I was really getting tired of passing out and then waking up somewhere else. There was commotion all around me but I'm not sure whether it was the noise or the burning pain in my shoulders that woke me up. I opened my eyes only to find that I appeared to have been transported to Egypt, or at least behind the scenes for a dress rehearsal of *Aida*.

I was in a large warehouse space that had been transformed to look like something right out of Giza. Along the back wall were life-sized wooden or cardboard cut outs of palm trees and the silhouette of the pyramids in the distance. Closer to the foreground on the side wall, was a partial 3-D replica of the Sphinx. A wide set of stairs led up to the raised stage area, where I found myself secured by chains between two pillars, my arms raised above my head. No wonder my shoulders were aching after having to support most of my weight while I was unconscious. I was luckily able to get my feet underneath me and take my weight, relieving the strain on my arms. The chains securing me to the pillars now hung loosely but a quick test proved they were well secured. I wasn't going anywhere.

I looked around the stage area. It appeared to be modelled after the entrance to a temple, the pillars and faux stone archways etched with hieroglyphics. There were several large sarcophagi off to the far side of the stage where there also appeared to be some sort of brazier. The centerpiece of the stage was a statue of a green-skinned man holding what looked like a shepherd's crook and a whip or flail set high on a pedestal. I took a wild guess and figured it was supposed to be Osiris.

DiCastro had really gone all out for this little spectacle. There seemed to be a flurry of last minute preparations going on. I was just thinking that no one had noticed that I was awake when Holly stepped onto the stage.

I blinked in surprise, hardly recognizing her. She had changed her hair to jet black and styled it to look like Liz Taylor's Cleopatra, turquoise beaded braids hanging down on either side of her face. She was dressed similarly to me (I don't know what happened to the McQueen gown, I just hoped that I wasn't expected to return it) in a white sheath dress with straps at the shoulder and a high waist that gathered in under her breasts. It was more of a 'bought the slutty Cleopatra costume at the Halloween store look' than authentic ancient Egyptian attire though. The difference between our two outfits was that hers was made from a gauzy see-through material; it left little to the imagination. She was also adorned with several display cases worth of ancient Egyptian jewelry around her neck, wrists and upper arms.

"Good, you're awake. I'd hate for you to miss a moment of your impending death." The expression on her face was one of evil glee. She strode across the stage and frowned at me. "You," she said, gesturing to a passing man, dressed in an Egyptian kilt. "Tighten those chains."

The man disappeared behind me and the slack on the chains was pulled in, my arms raised above my head.

Holly sneered at me. "What's the matter Harry? No snippy comeback?"

I wish I could say I had a real zinger response, but all I came up with was, "You're not going to get away with this Holly." Yeah, lame I know, but it was all I had.

Holly laughed. "Really Harry, is that the best you can do?"

"No! No, no, no!" DiCastro's voice sounded angry, echoing across the empty space. I watched him cross the cavernous warehouse shaking his head. He was dressed like an Egyptian prince in a pleated, white kilt. His chest was bare and he wore gold cuffs on either wrist. Around his neck a wide, turquoise and gold ornamental necklace flashed in the light. He had a large ceremonial dagger tucked into the front of his kilt and I recognized it as the same one from Bryce's video. He was followed by several similarly, although less extravagantly, clad men. I glanced at Holly as she watched him draw closer and the expression on her face alternated between love-sick puppy and fearful, abused wife. "No, it's all wrong. Where is the altar?" DiCastro stormed up the steps to the stage followed by his entourage.

"Levy, my love. What's the matter?" Holly approached him demurely. She reached for his arm only to have him brush her off.

"I told you to prepare her for the ritual." He turned to glare at me, the dark kohl lines under his eyes giving him a menacing look.

"I..," Holly stammered.

"Where is the altar?" DiCastro interrupted as if Holly hadn't even spoken. He turned to two of his cronies. "Find the altar back stage and bring it out." He swung back to look at me, his eyes lingering on my body. I was very glad my dress was not as see-through as Holly's. He turned back to look at Holly, truly seeing her for the first time. "Your hair looks ridiculous," he said with a scowl.

Holly patted her hair nervously. "I'm sorry, my love. I thought you would enjoy the look for the ceremony." Her hair slowly morphed back to her beach bunny blonde. She had a look in her eye like a beaten dog. I *almost* felt sorry for her.

DiCastro grunted at the change and then eyed the rest of Holly's costume critically. "Give me your necklace." He held out his hand.

Holly's hand flew to the gold jewelry she wore about her neck. It was shaped like a snake biting its own tail. "I...I thought..."

"That's the problem. You're not supposed to think." DiCastro scowled at her as she unclasped the necklace and handed it to him. "This is the necklace for the bride of Osiris." He moved to fasten the necklace around my neck.

"The bride?" Holly looked confused. "But I am to be...."

A commotion from behind interrupted her as four men pushed a large wheeled dolly carrying an altar block across the stage. The altar had been made up to look like a single chiseled stone with iron rings sunk into the surface at the four corners. DiCastro smiled when he saw it. "Perfect," he said. "Move it over here, then secure the girl to it. We must prepare to start the ritual the moment the sun has set. At the anointed time I will mount the altar and take my chosen bride, then sacrifice her heart to the god."

Oh joy. I wasn't just going to be murdered by a crazy person, I was going to be raped and murdered by a crazy person. Could it get any worse?

"But Levy, I don't understand." Holly reached out to stop him. "I am to be your bride, not her." She looked at me with venom. "Why would you want to fuck her?"

DiCastro laughed and grabbed Holly by the throat, his hand cutting off her airway as he pulled her close, face to face. Holly scrabbled at his hand, her feet barely touching the floor, her face turning red. "You're right, you stupid cow. You don't understand." He shook her like a rag doll. "You were never anything but an easy fuck and a means to an end." He drew the dagger out from his waist.

"No!" I shouted, realizing what he was about to do. "DiCastro, stop." I couldn't help myself. No matter how betrayed I felt by Holly, I didn't want her dead. I pulled at the chains holding my arms and kicked out at the nearest man as he approached me.

DiCastro began to mutter an incantation and the dagger started to glow. Suddenly, he plunged it into Holly's stomach. He released her throat and she bent double over the blade then slid to the floor.

"No! Holly!" Tears stung my eyes.

DiCastro stood over Holly's body and took a deep breath. A wave of power rippled over him and the look on his face was ecstatic. "Yes! I can feel that worthless bitch's power. It's mine now." He turned to look at me and smiled. "Just like yours soon will be, my bride." He brought the dagger to his lips and licked Holly's blood from the edge. "Clean up this trash and prepare the girl. We begin at sundown."

I watched in horror as he strode away across the stage, revulsion sending shivers down my spine. For the first time since waking up after being translocated from Dante's, I began to feel truly defeated. How would I ever get out of this nightmare?

Chapter Twenty-four

I admit I sort of zoned out for a while after Holly's death. It was too much of a shock to process everything and I think my brain just sort of shut down for a bit. I don't even remember struggling when the men released the chains from the pillar and reshackled me spread-eagle on the altar.

I'm not sure how long I lay there when I realized that the sounds around me were getting louder. Dozens of people, all dressed in Egyptian attire, had begun to fill the space around the stage, milling about and murmuring.

A man, dressed in the robes of an Egyptian priest, walked across the stage and lit the large brazier. The flame sprang to life just as a gong sounded from somewhere behind me. The priest raised his arms in benediction and the crowd grew silent. Quietly at first, then growing louder and more fervent, the crowd began to chant, "Asar, Asar." Over and over again they chanted the name of their god. The chanting became frenzied as DiCastro stepped out from behind the statue of Osiris, flanked by two jacks.

He stood in front of the crowd at centre stage and raised his arms. The crowd instantly fell silent.

"My friends!" DiCastro's voice echoed through the large space; he must have been using magic to enhance the sound. "My friends, tonight you are present to witness the birth of a new regime; a new power for Riverton, for the world!"

The crowd cheered. Clearly they had also been drinking the *Kool-aid* in copious quantities.

"It is the night of the new moon. A night for rebirth, when we will see our Lord Asar restored to his rightful place on this plane."

Another crazed cheer erupted from the crowd and DiCastro paused for a moment, basking in the adulation.

"Years of planning and preparing have all come down to this night. We have already made such great strides. Our numbers continue to grow, thanks in part to your recruitment and that is why you have been rewarded today the privilege of witnessing our Lord Asar's rebirth."

More crazy fan applause followed this pronouncement. DiCastro motioned to four men dressed as priests who proceeded to join him on stage.

"And thanks to our brothers, who have lent their talents and skill to help us begin to assemble our army, an army that will defeat not only the mongrels but the bloodsuckers as well."

The crowd cheered loudly as the four men raised their arms. Suddenly I was overcome by the sense of dread that I had learned to associate with the appearance of zombies. Sure enough, from the side of the cavernous space by the Sphinx, a door opened and an army of zombies shuffled out, two by two. There must have been close to a hundred of them. They shambled along, their gait closer to a walk than a shuffle. The mages that had raised these zombies were getting better at it and were exhibiting impressive control over their creations. The zombies stopped behind the crowd giving the appearance of standing at attention. The cheer from the crowd this time was somewhat subdued as the people gathered around the stage eyed the zombies cautiously.

"Don't be alarmed my friends," DiCastro continued, sensing the crowd's unease. "Our army of undead will protect us from outside interference as we begin the ritual." He raised his arms again in benediction. "Join me now my friends. Join me in prayer as we call to our fallen Lord, so that he might rise again."

DiCastro began to chant in a foreign tongue. Having never heard ancient Egyptian, I can only guess that that's what it was. Soon the crowd fell into step, carrying the chant along. After about five minutes, DiCastro lowered his arms and signalled to the four men again. He turned and sat on a throne that I hadn't noticed before, carved into the base of the statue of Osiris. The crowd continued to chant, some of them with their hands in the air, swaying to the tempo of the chanting. The air around the stage began to feel thick, the magic being released by the incantation almost palpable. I could feel their zealous frenzy building and I sucked the power into myself greedily.

The four men moved across the stage and returned a few minutes later, each dragging an obviously drugged person along with them. Judging from their dress and general grubby appearance, they were some of the missing homeless. They came to a stop in a line in front of DiCastro who rose to his feet, the Dagger of Asar raised above his head. He began to chant again, his voice booming out over the drone of words coming from the crowd below the stage.

When he approached the first man to be sacrificed, I closed my eyes not wanting to witness what was about to happen. But that's when it hit me, someone needed to witness the atrocities that were about to occur. I owed it to these poor people who trusted Holly and were betrayed by her just as badly as I was, only to be slaughtered by a lunatic with aspirations of god-hood.

I opened my eyes just as DiCastro drew the dagger across the first man's throat. There was a momentary lucid look of surprise in the man's eyes, as the arterial spray of blood splashed across DiCastro, then he slumped to the floor. DiCastro raised his arms in triumph as a wave of power rushed into his body, his ecstatic, blood covered face a macabre sight.

The grisly scene was repeated three more times until nothing on the stage was left untouched by the spray of blood, including me. With each new kill, the magical energy multiplied. I could feel it throbbing like a beating heart. My face was spattered with blood and I licked my lips without thinking, only to be rewarded with a rush of power like I had never felt before. The warm, coppery taste was euphoric. It sizzled against my tongue, as I drew the magical power into my core. It was like nothing I had ever experienced. I closed my eyes against the onslaught of feelings warring inside me, euphoria with a large chaser of guilt. How could I be enjoying any part of this slaughter? What was wrong with me? The sight of blood should have sickened me but instead I hungered for it.

My mouth suddenly ached, the pain almost excruciating. I opened my mouth, flexing my jaw like I was yawning to try and alleviate the pain. When I closed my mouth again, my tongue brushed against something that hadn't been there before. What the hell? Since when did I have fangs?

"*Harry! Harry! Can you hear me?*"

Great. Now I was hearing voices too. I looked around frantically. DiCastro and his cronies were still basking in the glow of their latest kill. There was no one else nearby.

"*Harry, what's happening?*"

"*Isaac? Isaac is that you?*"

"*Yes Harry, it's me. Something has happened. Why are you suddenly so strong? I could feel you faintly before but now you are shining like a beacon.*"

"*I don't know. DiCastro is performing some sort of blood magic. It's...it's affecting me somehow. You have to help me Isaac. He's going to kill me.*"

"*We're on our way Harry. Hold on. And....and try not to drink any blood.*"

"*Too late. I licked some off my lip. It tasted so good and now I have fangs. Fangs! What the hell is happening to me?*"

"*It's okay Harry. I'll explain everything to you. Just hang on. We're almost there.*"

"*I hope you brought the cavalry because there are over a hundred zombies on guard duty.*"

"*The cavalry is coming. Nash says you better be in one piece when he gets there or he'll kill you himself.*" I laughed at that, in spite of everything. It was obviously impossible for Nash not to bully me.

The temporary feeling of relief I had that a rescue was on its way, was short lived. When I opened my eyes again, I was startled to find DiCastro standing beside me. His skin was red with the blood of his victims, his face frozen in a rictus grin. With total revulsion I realized that his free hand was moving rhythmically under his kilt, wrapped around his erection. He ran the dagger slowly down my chest, slipping it under the dress to cut the fabric apart, exposing my breasts.

"Soon my bride, soon the moon will reach its zenith and we will become one with the god." He leered at my breasts then ran the dagger back up towards my face, wiping the blood off the blade on my cheek and lips.

"The only thing you are going to become one with is your own death, you crazy asshat." I turned my head away from the sight of him, just as a warning bell began to sound.

"No! No, there are intruders in the building," DiCastro turned and yelled at the jacks that until this point had remained motionless on the stage. "Stall them. We need more time to complete the ritual."

The jacks moved with uncanny speed across the stage and disappeared from sight.

"Isaac, if you can still hear me, look out, there are two jacks coming your way." I could only hope that Isaac still had a channel open to me and heard my warning.

"You're too late DiCastro. You don't have enough power to complete the ritual."

"No, I won't be stopped." DiCastro glared at me with a crazed look in his eyes then turned to the priests. "The zombies, use the zombies and kill them all." His hand swept out over the chanting crowd. "I can channel their deaths. It will be enough power for the ritual."

The zombie masters moved to the edge of the stage. A few of the closest chanters must have heard DiCastro's words, because they began to panic and try to escape from the mob. The zombies moved in, tearing the chanters apart. Blood and gore splashed across the floor and the chanting was soon replaced by screams of pain and terror.

DiCastro stood with his arms raised, a look of ecstasy on his face, as he drank in the death magic. There was a momentary pause when a commotion broke out at the back of the building and a door burst open. A stream of vampires and werewolves, many in their deadly half-were form, rushed in.

"Kill them! Kill them all!" DiCastro screamed at the four priests, pointing at my rescuers.

The zombies turned and began to attack the werewolves and vampires.

"No!" I shouted, searching the crowd for a familiar face. Where was Tess? Where were Isaac and Nash? I struggled against the shackles holding me down on the altar, anger pulsing through me.

Suddenly, a half-were burst through the door locked in battle with one of the jacks. For some reason I knew that it was Nash. His half-were form was impressive, over seven feet tall and all muscle and claws covered in a thick, dark fur. He was bleeding from multiple wounds and appeared to be favouring his left arm. The jack looked like it had taken a beating, but wounds wouldn't slow it down. The two combatants faced off, oblivious to the chaos around them.

"They're too late," DiCastro crowed, pulling my attention away from the fight. He heaved himself onto the altar, straddling my hips. "Your powers will be mine." He fumbled with my skirt pushing it up my legs. He pushed his own kilt aside exposing his now flaccid penis. He began to stroke himself vigorously with one hand, grabbing my breast and squeezing it painfully with the other.

"Nash!" I screamed in panic and bucked my hips trying to dislodge him. There was no way this was happening. I struggled against my bonds, throwing all my strength against the metal shackles.

"Harry!" Nash's voice carried across the chaos. "Hang on, Harry." I turned my head to see that Nash was moving closer, trying to cross the space, but the jack was in pursuit, slowing him down.

"Harry, the zombies, use your powers." Isaac's voice whispered in my head.

Of course! Why didn't I think of that? I looked across the large space. There were still over half of the zombies left, battling with the dozen or so werewolves and vampires. If I could send the zombies back where they came from, the battle would be over. I closed my eyes and tried to push everything out of my head and just focus on the zombies. It was easier said than done with DiCastro masturbating on top of me. Luckily, after having a hard-on for the last hour, he seemed to be experiencing a technical difficulty.

I focused on the zombies and pictured them returning to dust. Taking a deep breath, I tried to slowly release my will but my body was supercharged after all the magic I had absorbed during DiCastro's ritual, so rather than the focused stream I had intended, it burst from me and roared across the entire space. The zombies exploded into dust and the cavernous room fell eerily silent.

An aftershock of power rocked the stage and the altar shook like it was an earthquake, tossing DiCastro off me to the floor. One of the pillars toppled over nearly landing on the altar and in that moment I felt the power resurging through me like a shot of adrenaline. I pulled against my restraints, the magic coursing through me as first one, then the other, tore free from the altar, the shackles still bound to my wrists, the eye-ring bolts they had been attached to dangling uselessly.

"Noooooo! No! You can't stop me!" DiCastro sprang to his feet, his eyes glazed like a mad man's.

"You bitch! This is all your fault." He pulled the dagger from his kilt and lunged at me.

I put my arms up to ward off the blow and the dagger connected with one of the shackles on my wrist and then bounced off, slicing a shallow line down my forearm. He lunged again and I caught his wrist, the dagger inches from my chest, but my legs were still spread-eagled on the altar and I couldn't get any leverage. There was a loud growl and a huge, furry black wolf streaked between DiCastro and me, taking him down to the floor. I watched in shock as the giant wolf tore DiCastro's throat out. The wolf shook his head and sneezed like he had tasted something unpleasant, then turned and looked at me, his muzzle dripping with DiCastro's blood.

"Uh, nice wolf. Good wolf." I gestured for the wolf to keep down. "Nash?"

The wolf sniffed at me then tilted his head back and howled. Across the warehouse, the other wolves responded. Nash, or at least the wolf I was pretty sure was Nash, jumped up on the altar and I fell back in surprise. His big nose sniffed at my face and then he started licking my cheek.

"Hey! Stop that." I made a face, pushing his big, shaggy head away and wiped the wolf slobber off my cheek. The big brute plunked himself down between my legs and sat, and I swear he smiled at me, his big wolfy tongue lolling from his bloodied muzzle. That's when I noticed that the front of my dress was still wide open and my breasts were on full display. I grabbed the remnants of the dress and clutched them to my chest. The wolf huffed at me, the equivalent of a wolfy laugh.

"You big, hairy pervert," I replied.

"Harry!" I turned to see Tess making her way across the floor. She was battered and bruised but okay.

"Tess! Thank god you're all right."

As Tess drew near, the wolf jumped to his feet and started to growl. Tess stopped in her tracks and dipped her head low in submission.

"Hey, stop that." I rested my hand on the wolf's shoulder.

"I don't think your wolf protector is going to let anyone else get close to you for a while," Isaac said as he approached from the other side of the stage. He looked rather worse for wear, his clothes in tatters.

"What took you so long?" I looked at Isaac and smiled.

"I had a bit of a disagreement with a jack and several zombies." Isaac frowned and looked at me critically. "Is any of that blood yours?"

"Just a scratch on my arm." Suddenly, a thought occurred to me. "The jacks! There must be two spirit walkers back in the infirmary. We have to get them before they get away."

"Already taken care of," Tess replied. "They wouldn't let me be part of the main rescue party since I couldn't go wolf this far from the full moon, but they let me be part of the secondary team. We rounded up the jack pilots and found the rest of the kidnapped homeless. No sign of Holly though."

My breath caught in my throat. I had forgotten about Holly and Tess didn't know what had happened. I felt tears in my eyes. The wolf whined and licked my face. "Oh Tess, Holly's dead," I said.

"Good. Saves me from having to kill the bitch," Tess all but growled.

"What? You know?" I looked at her in surprise.

"That she turned out to be a back-stabbing, traitorous slut? Yeah, I know."

"DiCastro killed her. He was just using her to get to me." I frowned at Tess. "But how did you know?"

"It was Bryce that figured it out. He found out that Holly had a secret email account and he uncovered months' worth of emails between her and DiCastro, emails where she gave him all our personal information and bitched about having to pretend to still like us."

My heart felt heavy with Holly's betrayal. I just wanted to go home and put the whole nightmare behind me. "Do you think you can find a key or something and get me out of here?" I shook a shackle at Isaac.

Isaac reached into his suit jacket's breast pocket - leave it to a vampire to wear a suit to a fight - and pulled out his lock pick tools. "Allow me." He moved towards the altar. The wolf turned his head and growled. "That is, if your protector will let me near."

"Come on Nash. Let Isaac unlock these damn restraints. I just want to go home." I ran my hand through his thick, coarse fur. The wolf gave my face another lick then sat down in agreement.

"Yeah, let's go home," said Tess.

And so we did, leaving the vampires and werewolves to clean up the mess and deal with any of the survivors. Other than the innocent homeless, I really didn't care what happened to the rest of the people. As far as I was concerned they were all crazy and just as guilty as DiCastro. After all, they willingly and actively participated in the whole shit-show right up until DiCastro turned the zombies on them.

Chapter Twenty-five

Tess took charge the moment we arrived home. Isaac had dropped us off in his big *Escalade* and then returned to oversee the cleanup at the warehouse. The wolf had curled up beside me on the bench seat in the back of the SUV and I have to admit, it was rather comforting to have him there, my fingers twined in his fur. Way better than having the human Nash grumbling and growling at me.

Tess sent me off to take a shower and hose all the blood off while she filled the big soaker tub in the bathroom. The wolf padded up the stairs beside me, but I adamantly insisted that he did not need to sit watching me in the shower, or at least I wasn't going to let him. I wasn't sure how long Nash had to stay in his wolf form after shifting. I knew that some shifters couldn't switch from their animal shape for at least several hours, but I suspected that Nash was a powerful enough alpha that he could have switched back whenever he wanted. He also wasn't fooling me with the whole 'I'm just like a big friendly dog' routine. I knew that Nash was still in there.

It felt great to clean all the blood and grime off, but I was really looking forward to a long hot soak, so I jumped out of the shower, wrapped myself in a towel and hustled into the bathroom the moment Tess called to say it was ready. The wolf was nowhere to be seen. I figured he had tired of playing guard dog so I was surprised to find him in my tub. That is to say Nash, the man, was in my tub.

"Hey! That's supposed to be my bath." I scowled at him. He was reclined at one end of the huge tub, his arms spread wide, resting on the marble edge, the water, complete with bubbles, lapped at his chest. Unlike his canine counterpart, the man-Nash had only a light dusting of hair on his chest, the water giving it a darker, curlier appearance. He had several long, angry, red scars across his left shoulder and chest. They were healing and looked weeks old rather than just mere hours. Chalk one up for werewolf metabolism.

"There's plenty of room," he replied with a smirk.

"Uh, no thanks." I turned to leave, my cheeks burning.

"Chicken."

For some reason, after everything that had happened, I just couldn't bring myself to ignore the challenge in his tone. I turned and faced the tub, letting the towel drop, then climbed in at the opposite end. The water was borderline too hot, just the way I liked it, and I couldn't help but sigh in relief as I slid down until the water was at my chin. Nash's hands skimmed over my legs as he guided them to either side of his, sending a shiver up my spine.

"Keep your hands to yourself, buster," I said.

Nash laughed and held his hands up in surrender, but any comment he may have made was interrupted when Tess barged through the door, a plate piled with sandwiches and a container of chocolate milk in her hands. She was freshly showered and wearing a kimono-type robe, her wet hair wrapped in a towel.

She did a little double take at the sight of Nash sharing my tub, hiding a smile while she busied herself with delivering the food.

"Here, peanut butter and jelly. Eat up. I'm sure you need to refuel." She set the plate down on the marble tub surround between Nash and me.

Nash immediately grabbed a sandwich. "What kind of jelly?"

"Hey! Those are my sandwiches!" I flicked the water at him with my fingers.

"Strawberry," replied Tess.

"Good. That's the only way to go." Nash took a big bite and smiled a wolfish smile.

"Yeah, I've heard that somewhere before," I grumbled, grabbing a sandwich of my own. "Thanks, Tess."

"No problem, Harry," she replied, her face taking on a sad expression. "I was so worried about you. Don't ever do that to me again!" She reached over and hugged my head to her chest.

"Mmmph!" I replied, my mouth full of peanut butter; plus, it was very had to talk when being suffocated against someone's chest. I sort of let out a little yelp and Tess released her grip.

"Sorry." She smiled sheepishly. "Oh! I almost forgot." She reached into her pocket and pulled out her cellphone. "You've got a call."

"On *your* phone?" I guess it made sense since I had no clue where my phone ended up. Hopefully it was back at Dante's with the rest of my clothes. I grabbed the phone from Tess. "Hello?"

"Ah, my dear Angharad, so good to hear your voice."

"Salvador."

"Isaac tells me that you are well, is this so?"

"I'm fine."

"Wonderful. I am so relieved to hear it. Your assistance in dealing with our little zombie problem was much appreciated." Little zombie problem? Seriously?

Who was he kidding? "I look forward to hearing of your adventure when next we see each other."

"Uh, sure." I really had no interest in reliving the whole *adventure* for Salvador's entertainment, but I doubted I would have much choice.

"In the meantime," Salvador continued on, "I have taken the liberty of sending a small token of my appreciation for your assistance."

"That really wasn't necessary," I cringed thinking about the McQueen dress, "and, well, I'm sorry, but the dress is totally ruined."

"Not to worry my dear, there are more where that came from." That's what I was afraid he was going to say.

"Okay. Well, thanks."

"Good night, or should I say, good morning, Harry."

"Good night, Salvador."

It wasn't until I hung up the phone and handed it back to Tess that I realized he had called me Harry. Was it a good thing or a bad thing that I was now on a first name basis with the scariest vampire in town?

"Well, I guess you don't need any more help from me," Tess said. She eyed Nash who was helping himself to my chocolate milk and grinned.

"Uh, no. I think I can manage. That is, if wolfman over there doesn't hog all the milk."

Tess left and I finished off my sandwiches, washing them down with the last of the milk. I lay back and closed my eyes with a sigh.

"Do you want to talk about what happened?" Nash's voice was quiet.

"Not really."

"Okay."

I heard the water slosh as he stood and climbed out of the tub. I was too tired to even take a peek. Honest.

He puttered around a few minutes drying himself - I kept my eyes closed the whole time - and then he padded out of the bathroom. I waited a few more minutes then sighed, before opening the drain and climbing out of the tub.

Back in my bedroom I intended on just falling into bed, but it was already taken.

"You can't sleep here," I said to Nash, who was occupying the far side, *my side*, of the bed.

Nash just looked at me and pulled back the covers enough to let me in. "Get in," he ordered.

"Look, I don't want to have sex with you." I felt awkward standing there in just a towel.

"I don't want to have sex with you either," he replied, his tone implying mild exasperation.

"Then what are you doing in my bed? I don't need to f-feed." It was true, but I hated that expression. I had taken on so much power during the ritual that even with my massive expenditure to banish the zombies, I still felt fully charged. "You don't even like me," I muttered somewhat petulantly.

Nash huffed out a little breath, running his hand through his hair. "Look, the wolf is still upset about what happened. He needs to be close."

"Fine," I said, rolling my eyes. "Just stay on your side of the bed."

***

The next morning, or maybe it was already afternoon, I awoke to find myself alone in bed. Sighing with relief that an awkward moment was avoided, I got dressed and followed the smell of bacon downstairs.

When I walked around the corner and into the kitchen, two things hit me. First, out of habit, I had expected to see Holly in her usual place cooking breakfast. The pain of her betrayal felt like a knife in my stomach all over again. Second, Nash was wearing a frilly apron and cooking bacon and eggs.

"Good morning," I said.

"Morning, just barely," he replied, expertly cracking an egg onto the griddle. "How do you like your eggs?"

"Over easy I guess."

Nash grunted and pushed a glass of orange juice at me. "Sit down and drink up. Breakfast will be ready in a few minutes."

I guess the wolf wanted to see me fed as well. I could work with that. The aroma of bacon was making my stomach growl.

"Have you seen Tess?" I asked, the house suddenly feeling empty.

"She had to go into work." Nash turned and put some bread in the toaster. "She left you a note." He pointed to a slip of paper hanging on the fridge.

I grabbed the note and gave it a quick read. All it said was '*Back at 5. We need a movie night. I'll pick up pizza. Make lots of popcorn. WTF the truck?*'

I starred at Tess's note in confusion. I had no clue what that last bit was about. Nash looked at me and shrugged.

"You better look out back," he said and then turned back to the grill. He plated up some hashbrowns, bacon and two eggs and set the plate in front of me. "But don't take too long or your breakfast will get cold."

I slid off the stool and hurried over and threw open the door. There beside my old beater of a truck was a brand new Ford F-150. It was metallic green and had a great big bow on top of the hood.

"A truck? A new truck is a small token of appreciation?" Well, I guess it was better than another expensive dress.

***

Later that night, after we all but demolished two large pizzas, a case of beer and a bowl of popcorn, and binged on the entire original *Star Wars* trilogy (I'm talking episodes IV to VI), Tess excused herself for bed, leaving me alone with Isaac. Nash had taken off right after breakfast and the awkward moment I thought I had avoided earlier made an appearance. I hadn't heard from him since. Not that I expected to.

"So do you think what DiCastro was trying to do would have worked?" I asked Isaac. I really didn't know whether I believed if a god, any god, existed.

"No." He steepled his fingers in front of his chin. For movie night he had gone all casual and he wore black dress pants and a silky dark, almost black, purple, button front shirt. This was completely different than my definition of casual which was why I was wearing a one piece pair of flannel pajamas. With feet.

"You don't believe the gods exist?" I asked.

"No, it's not that. It's just he would never have succeeded because he would not have been able to kill you."

"Uh, hello? He was going to shove a six inch dagger through my heart. I'm pretty sure he would have killed me."

"He may have facilitated your first death, but not your true death."

I looked at Isaac blankly. Say what?

"Tell me what happened when you tasted the blood last night," Isaac asked, appearing to change the subject.

"I don't know. I was getting high on all the magical energy in the room. The blood tasted so good and I..." I frowned, not really sure of what happened next. "Something happened and my whole mouth felt like it was cracking open or something. It was some sort of hallucination."

"A hallucination? You're sure that's all it was?"

"I thought for a minute I had fangs, Isaac. I'm pretty sure it was just my mind playing tricks." I bared my teeth to him. "Thsee? No fangths."

Isaac raised his eyebrows at me, a smirk on his face. "No fangs now, but what about then?"

"No, it was just a weird hallucination. Why would I suddenly sprout fangs?"

"You can't think of anyone you know, anyone with a beating heart mind you, that has fangs?"

"Well there's Tomas, but he's...." I trailed off thinking about what Isaac was getting at. I had learned that Tomas was a dhamphir, the living offspring of a vampire and a human. "You can't mean?"

Isaac shrugged again. "If the tooth fits."

I shook my head trying to deny the truth that had been staring me in the face for a while. My father, whoever he was, was a vampire.

The End.

Thank you for reading Dead and Kicking. I hope you enjoyed reading it as much as I did writing it. As an independent author, I rely on word of mouth to help sell books. If you are so inclined, please consider leaving a review online at your favourite bookseller's website.

I would also like to take this opportunity to thank all my beta readers. Thanks for your fresh eyes, suggestions and advice. I take full responsibility for any mistakes that remain.

Don't miss a thing! Keep up with all the news and receive exclusive offers and content by joining my mailing list. Visit my website at www.lisaemme.com and sign up today!

Cheers!
Lisa

Coming Soon!

Harry's story continues. Her next book is available now for pre-order at your favourite authorized retailer.

Tooth and Claw - The Harry Russo Diaries, volume 2

Q: When is a witch, not a witch?
A: When she's a necromancer.

Angharad 'Harry' Russo has had to adjust to some major changes in her life. Her computer is haunted, she accidentally acquired a vampire servant and she's attracted to the most aggravating alpha male on the planet. Her friend betrayed her, a lunatic tried to sacrifice her to raise a god and she accidentally 'outed' herself to the Magister, the most powerful vampire in town. What else could go wrong? Oh yeah, she's just discovered that her father is a vampire and her dhamphiric powers are emerging prematurely. Poor Harry doesn't know what weird ability could pop up next.

When werewolves start to go missing, and two young men die suspiciously, not to mention horrifically, Harry believes it's all connected. It could be just a hunch, or it could be the big, grey wolf that stepped out of her dreams to haunt her waking moments; either way, Harry knows that she needs to help solve the mystery. Now if she could just convince the sexy police detective, Cian Nash, to take her seriously.

About the Author

Lisa Emme is a Canadian who proudly ends her ABC's with 'zed'. A self-professed book-a-holic, she has spent the last few years trying to stem her book hoarding tendencies by writing her own stories and by avoiding the bargain table at the bookstore like the plague.

A bit of a thrill seeker, Lisa has tried such death defying activities as bungy jumping off a bridge and rappelling down the side of a 17 storey building. She's also single-handedly raising a teenager.

Lisa has worked as a veterinary assistant, playground instructor, bank teller, store clerk, waitress, telephone solicitor, research writer for an environmental think tank, computer programmer, and systems analyst. Her passion however, is writing. What else is she going to do during the long, cold prairie winter?

Lisa would love to hear from you.

You can find her here:

Website: www.lisaemme.com
Facebook: www.facebook.com/LisaEmmeBooks
E-mail: lisa.emme@mymts.net

Made in the USA
Middletown, DE
05 July 2016